DID HE DO IT ON PURPOSE?

Callie gasped as George grabbed for the phone. "No, no, I insist!" he exclaimed, pulling the phone out of her grip. "I'll just call the stable, and then I'll help you—oops!"

Callie gasped again, watching as the cell phone slid out of George's grip and flew up in a wide arc before falling toward the streambed. Snapping out of her trancelike state, she lunged for it, trying to catch it before it hit the ground. But she was too late. The phone smashed against the rocky slope, a large piece of the black plastic casing snapping off and whizzing to the ground. The rest of the phone bounced, landing a split second later with a splash in the stream, which swept it away.

"Ohmigosh! I'm sorry!" George's gray eyes were wide. "It slipped, Callie, I swear! I'm really sorry."

Callie's heart was pounding at triple its usual speed. Suddenly she was completely certain that George wasn't sorry. He'd done it on purpose—all of it. First he'd followed her into the woods, far from civilization. Then he'd found a way to put her horse out of commission. And now he'd effectively removed her last link with anyone who could help her.

PINE HOLLOW®

HEADSTRONG

BY BONNIE BRYANT

BANTAM BOOKS
NEW YORK • TORONTO • LONDON • SYDNEY • AUCKLAND

Special thanks to Sir "B" Farms and Laura Roper

RL 5.0, AGES 012 AND UP

HEADSTRONG
A Bantam Book/October 2000

ISBN: 0-553-49304-3

Visit us on the Web! www.randomhouse.com
Educators and librarians, for a variety of teaching tools, visit us at
www.randomhouse.com/teachers

Published simultaneously in the United States and Canada

Bantam Books is an imprint of Random House Children's Books. BANTAM
BOOKS and the rooster colophon are registered trademarks of Random
House, Inc. Bantam Books, 1540 Broadway, New York, New York 10036.

PRINTED IN THE UNITED STATES OF AMERICA
OPM 10 9 8 7 6 5 4 3 2 1

My special thanks to Catherine Hapka
for her help in the writing of this book.

ONE

Callie Forester squinted at the sun, its dull yellow-white form visible through a break in the trees on the trail just ahead. It was beginning to sink through the leaden winter sky toward the western horizon, which meant that Callie had been riding for several hours. It was time to head home. Spying a wide spot on the wooded trail, she reluctantly reversed direction and then gently nudged the Arabian gelding she was riding and clucked to send him into a trot. Barq shook his head and complied, though his trot was a little choppier than usual.

"It's okay, boy. We're heading home now," Callie murmured, her attention not really as focused on the horse as it should have been. She was too busy thinking about that day's ride. It hadn't gone as well as she'd hoped, and she hadn't been hoping for a whole lot. She had been training on Barq for almost three weeks. While the Arabian gelding was a popular and reliable lesson horse at Pine Hollow Stables,

Callie had already accepted the fact that he was never going to be the endurance horse of her dreams. She had been a junior endurance champion before moving to Willow Creek, Virginia, some six months earlier—or rather, before the serious car accident that had injured her soon after the move—and now that her body had finally healed, she couldn't wait to get back in the game. The trouble was, Barq was just about the only lesson horse at Pine Hollow that was at all adequate for endurance riding.

She sighed. How was she ever going to get back into top competitive shape with a horse that was merely adequate?

Before long, horse and rider emerged from the woods and the long, low main building of Pine Hollow came into view across the fields. But Callie wasn't looking at the stable, or at the neatly tended rings and paddocks and various smaller outbuildings that surrounded it. Instead she was focusing on the rambling white farmhouse atop a hill beyond the stable area. That was where Max Regnery, the owner of Pine Hollow, lived with his wife and two young daughters.

Maybe it was time for Callie to have another talk with Max about what to do. But what good would it do to discuss it again? Callie already knew that

2

Barq was the best endurance prospect in Max's stable. She already knew the only solution: to find a horse of her own, one that was suited to her ability, personality, and goals. Her parents had already agreed to the plan. All she had to do was find the right horse.

It should be an easy job, Callie thought, giving Barq an extra squeeze as his gait faltered slightly. *It's not as if there aren't plenty of horses around here. Probably a lot more than where we used to live.* Callie's family had moved to Willow Creek the previous summer from the West Coast to be closer to her congressman father's work. Callie had been anxious and resentful about the move at first, but she'd been pleasantly surprised to find that the countryside of northern Virginia was dotted with pastures full of horses. Still, being able to find a horse—or even a whole herd of horses—wasn't the same as being able to find the perfect endurance prospect. In fact, it felt a little like looking for a needle in a whole field full of haystacks.

Callie brought Barq to a walk as they crossed the fields. She didn't want to spend any more time than she had to cooling him out once she reached the stable. The more time she spent hanging around Pine Hollow, the better the chance that George Wheeler would find her.

"Pathetic," she muttered to herself so fiercely that Barq's ears swiveled back curiously. "Totally pathetic."

She knew she shouldn't let George get to her, but she couldn't help it. He had a way of bringing out the worst in her—the petty irritability and feelings of insecurity that she kept pretty well hidden most of the time. It hadn't been that way at first. When Callie had first realized that the shy, pudgy, hopelessly nerdy guy had a crush on her, she'd been flattered. She'd even gone out with him once, wondering if she'd been too superficial when she'd ignored guys like George in the past—if maybe she had been missing out on something special. After all, the two of them did have a lot in common. Both of them were juniors at a private school in Willow Creek called Fenton Hall. Both spent most of their free time in the saddle.

But it had soon become painfully obvious that it wasn't going to work out. Obvious to Callie, at least. George had seemed blissfully unaware of Callie's growing discomfort as he continued to shadow her around the barn, insist on walking her to just about every class at school, and generally follow her around like a lovesick puppy. But it had been getting harder and harder for Callie to conceal the fact that she wished he would just go away and leave her alone for good.

4

Like the other day, for instance, she thought. *When he showed up at that farm out on Highway Twelve, I was so mad at him, I might as well have been looking at a goat.*

She winced as she thought about it. What had that horse been like, anyway? Just about all she could recall was that he'd been a nice-looking Appaloosa gelding. Well-built and personable. She couldn't even remember his name. Sammy? Spooky?

"But I do remember his feet," she murmured. "They looked really solid. And I think his gaits were pretty good—especially his trot."

The more she thought about it, the angrier she felt at George. For all she knew, that Appaloosa might have been the perfect horse for her. And thanks to George, she could barely remember what the gelding looked like, let alone form an opinion about whether he might be worth considering.

Stop it, she told herself firmly as Barq drifted to the left and stretched his head toward an appetizing patch of weeds. *Blaming George is a waste. Besides, it's fixable. I'll just make an appointment to take another look at that horse.*

That made her feel a little better. "Come on, boy," she said, clucking to Barq as she steered him past the weeds and aimed him straight at the barn once again. "You'll have plenty to eat back in your stall. Let's just get there, okay?"

5

Fifteen minutes later Barq was munching on a flake of hay and Callie was walking down the wide aisle in the direction of the stable office. She wasn't sure she still had the number of the farm where she'd seen the Appaloosa, but she knew it would be in the stable's overstuffed Rolodex.

She heard voices as she approached the entryway that connected the U-shaped stable aisle of the building with the office, rest rooms, and other human-oriented areas. Lots of voices. Loud, laughing, squealing voices.

I wonder what's going on out there? she thought idly, most of her attention still focused on trying to remember more about the Appaloosa. *Scooter—that was his name. Wasn't it?*

She blinked and stopped short as she reached the end of the aisle, temporarily distracted from her thoughts. Usually the entryway was just that—a place to pass through on the way to other, more interesting parts of the stable. At that moment, though, it seemed to be the most popular spot in the place. Max was there, leaning on a rake and scratching his chin. So was Callie's older brother, Scott. He was in the middle of the crowd, laughing loudly and slapping Red O'Malley on the shoulder. Red was Pine Hollow's head stable hand. His longtime girlfriend, a petite, dark-haired, twenty-something stable hand named Denise McCaskill, was standing beside Red and smiling shyly at Carole Hanson, who was arm in arm with her new boyfriend, Cam Nelson. Stevie Lake and Lisa Atwood were huddled nearby with Max's wife, Deborah. Various other people were milling around as well, most of them talking at the top of their lungs.

"What's going on?" Callie asked uncertainly, stepping toward Ben Marlow, who was hanging back at the edge of the crowd. That was nothing unusual—Ben always seemed to be around the stable, lurking in the background, never taking part in anything involving his fellow humans if he could help it.

Ben glanced at her. He was holding a horse named Congo. The big, solid gelding was standing calmly, unfazed by the noise and commotion all around him, displaying the unflappable temperament that made him one of Max's most reliable lesson horses. "Uh, Red and Denise," Ben said in his usual gruff, succinct manner.

"What about them?" Callie asked as patiently as she could. She didn't have anything in particular against Ben, but his monosyllabic habits could be really irritating when it came to getting information out of him.

Before Ben could answer, Stevie raced over and grabbed Callie's arm so hard that it hurt. "Did you hear the news?" she shrieked. "Red and Denise are getting married!"

"Oh!" Now Callie understood all the excitement. Though she had been riding at Pine Hollow for only six months, she knew that Red and Denise had both worked there for years and that they'd been a couple for most of that time.

"They just made the announcement." Stevie was dragging Callie forward as she chattered excitedly. "Come on, they still haven't spilled all the juicy details. I don't want to miss a thing."

Callie smiled tolerantly. She'd liked Stevie from the first time she met her. Stevie was so open and friendly and fun-loving that it would be difficult *not* to like her. Allowing herself to be dragged, Callie soon found herself face to face with the bride-to-be.

"Hi, Denise," Callie said warmly. "I hear congratulations are in order. What a surprise!"

"Thanks, Callie." The pretty young stable hand smiled and pushed a strand of wavy dark hair off one slightly flushed cheek. "I can hardly believe this is happening myself. But thanks."

Callie tilted her head slightly. Was it just her imagination, or did Denise's smile seem slightly shaky? "Are you okay?" she blurted out before she realized what she was doing. "Um, I mean, I'm sure you're excited and all. I just thought . . . Well, never mind."

Stevie cocked an eyebrow at her. "What kind of a congratulations speech is that, Callie?" she joked.

"You're going to scare her out of getting married if you're not careful."

"That's my sister," Scott put in with a grin. "A true romantic."

"It's okay, guys," Denise said. "I know this is, you know, kind of a surprise for everyone. I'm still getting used to the idea myself."

Red heard her and turned to give her a significant look. "Since you mentioned surprises, um . . ." He slipped an arm around his fiancée's waist. "Do you want to . . . ?"

"I suppose there's no time like the present." Denise took a deep breath. She definitely looked nervous now. "As long as you're all here, we have another announcement to make."

Callie glanced at Stevie and the others, wondering what was coming. Stevie caught her glance and shrugged.

"What is it, Denise?" Lisa asked curiously.

Stevie chuckled. "I think you're going to have a hard time topping your last announcement."

"Oh, I don't know about that," Denise said. This time Callie could plainly see the nervousness in Denise's face. The stable hand cleared her throat and glanced at Red before turning back to her waiting audience. "You see, we just found out that I'm— um, I mean, *we're*—well, we're pregnant."

9

Callie's eyes widened. *Aha*, she thought. *That explains a lot.*

This time nobody seemed to know what to say. After a moment of silence, Max cleared his throat. "Er, I suppose this requires some additional congratulations, then," he said tactfully.

"Yeah," Stevie said. "So we're going to have a new little junior stable hand toddling around here soon. Cool!"

Denise shrugged and glanced over at Red again. "Well, it's not quite the way we'd planned," she said quietly.

"It never is." Max's wife, Deborah, spoke up, stepping over to give Denise a quick hug. "But don't worry about a thing, Denise. After our two girls, Max and I are practically experts at the whole childbirth thing. Not to mention professional-level babysitters."

"Thanks, Deborah." Denise gave the older woman a heartfelt smile. "I'm sure I'll have tons of questions for you. This is—well, let's just say we're feeling a little unprepared right now. Happy, of course. Just nervous."

Lisa eased over to join Callie and Stevie. "Wow," she murmured. "Talk about big news!"

"No kidding," Callie agreed, wondering exactly how happy Denise and Red really were about this turn of events. One of Callie's older cousins had become pregnant accidentally, and Callie still remembered the uproar it had caused in their family—and the cousin had already been engaged at the time.

Meanwhile, Red was still talking to the group at large. "We were thinking about getting married soon anyway," he explained. "Actually, we've been talking about it for almost a year now. This just means we need to pick up the pace a little."

"Yeah, like from a square halt straight to a Kentucky Derby gallop," Stevie muttered just loud enough for her friends to hear.

Carole heard the comment and giggled. She could hardly believe all the new developments. "Isn't this romantic?" she whispered to Cam, who was standing beside her with his arm resting casually across her shoulders. "Red and Denise have always been two of my favorite people in the whole world. I still remember how happy I was for them when they started going out—and now this! It's amazing."

"Uh-huh." Cam squeezed her shoulders a little tighter. "It's always great when two people can really connect like that." He leaned closer, his breath tickling her ear. "Sort of like us."

Carole shivered. She was tempted to pinch herself, but she was half afraid that if she did, she might wake up and discover that the wonderful adventure her life had become was all a dream. It was still

11

rather hard to believe, especially after the total disarray her life had been in only a few short weeks earlier. She had been grounded for cheating on a test at school, hardly speaking to her father, and banned from the things that gave her life meaning—horses and riding. She'd been forced to arrange for someone else to care for her horse, Starlight, while she was stuck at home studying. It had been the most miserable period of her life since the death of her mother years before.

But all that had changed. Now it was hard to imagine how things could get much better, and most of it was thanks to Cam. Even though he had been back in her life for only about a week, it was already difficult for her to imagine how she had lived without him. True, he hadn't been able to make her forget completely about all that other stuff. But New Year's was only a few weeks away, and Carole was sure that after that things would go back to normal.

No, better than normal, she told herself as she felt the weight of Cam's arm around her. *Much better than normal.*

In the meantime, she was doing all she could to enjoy the feeling—the wonderful, amazing, floating-on-air feeling—of being half of a couple. She had always felt a little bit awkward when the topic was romance, even with her longtime best friends Stevie and Lisa, mostly because the two of them had always been a lot more successful with guys than Carole had. Stevie had been dating a great guy named Phil Marsten ever since first meeting him at riding camp back in junior high. Lisa was so smart and beautiful that she'd never had any trouble attracting male attention, even before she had started dating Stevie's twin brother, Alex, the previous winter. And that was still true. When Lisa and Alex had decided to start seeing other people, Scott Forester—likable, popular Scott, who just happened to be one of the best-looking guys Carole had ever known—had almost immediately asked her out.

"So you still haven't told us when the big day is going to be," Stevie said to Red and Denise, breaking into Carole's thoughts. "The wedding, I mean."

Carole giggled. "That's just like Stevie," she whispered to Cam. "Why be subtle when you can be direct?"

Red and Denise exchanged quick looks. "Well, there's not really going to be a wedding," Red said haltingly.

"Huh?" Lisa blinked. "But you just said—"

"He just means there's not going to be a big, fancy kind of wedding," Denise explained. "We'll probably get married at home, or maybe down at the town hall. No big deal."

Carole couldn't believe her ears. How could such

a wonderful couple even imagine getting married in such an un-wonderful way? Denise and Red shared a cramped apartment over a dry cleaner's shop in downtown Willow Creek—hardly the spot for a romantic occasion like a wedding. Just about the only place that sounded less appealing was the dusty, underlit town hall. "But you have to have a wedding," she protested. "It just won't be the same without a white dress and all your friends and a cake—"

"Carole," Max began warningly. "It's their life. Their business."

"It's okay, Max," Denise said. "I know how she feels. Believe me, I never expected to be doing things this way. Neither of us did." She glanced over at Red, who nodded. "But the truth is, we just can't afford a fancy wedding right now. I'm sorry—I really wish you could all be with us to celebrate. But with the baby coming, we're on a pretty strict budget. We thought we'd try to do it on New Year's Eve, though. That will make it special—just in a quieter way."

New Year's Eve? Carole was a little surprised at that—the holiday was less than a month away. As far as she knew, most people took even longer than that to decide what kind of wedding dress they wanted, let alone to plan a whole wedding, simple or not.

Then she realized the significance of the tight timing. Since Denise was pregnant, she probably didn't want to wait too long. Carole took Cam's hand tightly in her own. It was kind of scary to think about Red and Denise starting off their married life with so little in the way of security—a too-small, too-dingy apartment, no money saved, and a baby on the way. What would she do if the same sort of thing ever happened to her and Cam?

Not that I have to worry about that yet, she thought, blushing even to be thinking about it. *All we've done is kiss. Well, that's just about all, anyway. . . .*

Max's voice pulled her back to the here and now. "I've got an idea," he said. "Sort of a wedding gift from me and Deborah." He glanced at his wife, who looked interested. "How about if we host a wedding for you?"

Denise gasped. "Oh, Max!" she exclaimed. "That's so generous. But—no, we couldn't possibly accept."

"No way," Red added firmly. "Thanks, boss. But we'll be okay."

Carole bit her lip, disappointed at the response. She couldn't imagine any more wonderful solution to the couple's problem than the one Max had suggested. What could she say to change their minds?

Before she could figure it out, Deborah spoke up. "Nonsense," she said briskly. "Max is right. We'd love to do it."

Denise looked worried. "But it's such a huge responsibility . . . and the money . . ."

Max chuckled. "Hey, we're not offering to rent the Kennedy Center or anything," he said. "But I'm sure we can manage a nice ceremony up at the house, then a party for all your friends."

"Whoo-hoo!" Stevie hooted. "Par-tay!"

Everyone laughed as Max shot Stevie a mock frown. "Of course, Deborah and I will have veto power over the guest list."

Carole grinned. She knew Max was just giving Stevie a hard time. "Say yes, guys," she urged Red and Denise. "Please? We all want to be there to see you two tie the knot."

Red cleared his throat and gazed at Denise for a long moment. "Well," he said at last, "how could we possibly say no?"

"You couldn't," Stevie said. "So you'd better say yes!"

That made everyone laugh again, including Red and Denise. "All right, all right," Denise said, raising her voice to be heard over the chuckles. "Then we will say yes—with many thanks."

"Good." Max looked pleased. "Then I suppose

we'd better start making plans! After all, New Year's is right around the corner."

As the others began chattering excitedly about the plans, Cam tugged gently on Carole's hand. "Let's duck out," he whispered. "I want to talk to you about something."

Carole hesitated. She really wanted to find out more about the upcoming wedding—and volunteer to help in any way she could. But as she met Cam's pleading gaze, she relented. "Okay." She followed as he ducked into the stable aisle.

Soon they were alone except for several horses, which were peering at them over the half doors of their stalls. Cam turned to face her, dropping her hand so that he could wrap his arms around her waist and bury his face in her neck.

Carole almost immediately felt herself sliding away on the wave of warmth and pleasure that overtook her whenever she and Cam were close. But she managed to keep her head, remembering the reason they were there. "Hey, wait a minute," she said rather breathlessly, gently pushing him away. "I thought you said we were going to talk."

"I know," Cam said, leaning close and blowing a stray dark curl off her cheek. "I just can't help myself when I'm alone with you. I've never felt like this with anyone else. I can't get enough of you, Carole."

Carole gulped, not certain how to respond. She was pretty sure she felt the same way, though their new relationship had been such a whirlwind that she'd hardly had time to catch her breath, let alone think too much about it. Still, she had no idea how to put her feelings into words the way Cam did. He always seemed to know the perfect, most wonderful, romantic way to express things, while she was generally left gasping for words.

Fortunately, this time Cam didn't seem to expect a response. "Anyway, you're right." He took half a step back, though his hands still rested lightly on her waist. "I wanted to talk to you about Christmas."

"What about it?" Carole was slightly relieved at the change of topic.

"I was thinking, since this will be our first holiday together, I want it to be really special," Cam said softly, his brown eyes never leaving her own. "Something we'll always remember, you know?"

"I'll definitely always remember it, because of you," Carole said shyly.

Cam smiled and leaned forward to give her a quick kiss on the tip of her nose. "Me too, beautiful," he said. "But wouldn't it be great to do something special, just the two of us? I was thinking we could get together in private, exchange gifts—the whole happy holidays thing."

"Okay." Carole hadn't really thought about

exchanging gifts. She was still getting used to the idea of having a boyfriend at all—especially such a handsome and sweet and charming one as Cam. She didn't want to take any chances of jinxing her own good fortune by peering too far into the future. "Um, when do you want to do it?"

"That's the problem." For the first time, Cam frowned. "My folks just told me we have to go visit my cousins in Louisiana. We're leaving on Christmas Day, and we'll probably be down there the whole week."

"Oh." Carole felt her heart contract in disappointment. A whole week without Cam? It sounded like forever. "Well, maybe we could do it before you go."

She winced as soon as she said it, realizing that she would have to do some fast shopping if she wanted to find anything special enough to express her new feelings for Cam. Besides that, she would have to convince her father that such a shopping trip was necessary, even though she was technically still grounded.

To her relief, Cam was shaking his head. "I'm not sure that'll work," he said. "I've got team meetings three nights this week, and then this weekend you said your dad's taking you into D.C. for the day. So it may have to wait until I get back. My folks are supposed to go to some party at my dad's boss's house on New Year's Eve, so we'll definitely be home by then at the latest. Why don't we say we'll do it then?"

"That sounds perfect." Carole was relieved. Now she would have plenty of time to figure out the perfect gift for Cam. Maybe her friends could advise her. "We can get together before the wedding."

"The wedding . . . ," Cam repeated blankly. "Oh, right! I almost forgot. Do you think we'll be invited to that?"

Carole blinked, surprised that he even had to ask. Then she reminded herself that Cam had been back in the area for only a short time. He had no way of knowing how close all the Pine Hollow regulars really were. "Of course we will," she assured him. "At least I will, for sure. And who else would I bring as my date?"

"Nobody, I hope, or I might die of jealousy," Cam said teasingly, pulling her close again. "Okay, then. We'll get together in the afternoon, before the wedding."

"Great." Carole closed her eyes as Cam leaned forward to kiss her again. But for once, she wasn't totally focused on the moment. She was already wondering how she could possibly find a gift special enough to express her feelings for Cam.

TWO

Lisa was so overwhelmed by the news of Red and Denise's engagement and pregnancy that she couldn't quite bring herself to leave the entryway, even as Max headed for the office, Red hurried off to teach an adult private lesson, and Denise and Deborah wandered toward the door, deep in a discussion about napkins and invitations. *It's amazing how fast things can change,* Lisa thought. *And usually when you're least expecting it.*

"What a day!" Stevie exclaimed in Lisa's ear, jolting her out of her thoughts. "Still, the Starlight Ride stops for no one. Anyone want to help me load wood into the trailer for the bonfire?" She gazed expectantly at Lisa and Callie. The Starlight Ride was a yearly event at Pine Hollow, a Christmas Eve trail ride followed by a bonfire in the town center. It was mostly for the younger riders, but this year Stevie had volunteered to help Max and his staff with the planning and preparations. She was also writing an article about the event for her school newspaper, the Fenton Hall *Sentinel.*

Callie glanced at her watch. "Maybe in a bit. I have to make a phone call. Catch you guys in a while, okay?" Without waiting for an answer, she headed toward the hall leading to the office and the pay phone.

"I'll come help you in minute," Lisa said, not quite ready to subject herself to Stevie's cheerful chatter just yet. She loved her friend dearly, but sometimes her boundless exuberance could be kind of exhausting, especially when Lisa had important issues on her mind. "Go ahead and I'll meet you outside."

"Okay, cool." Stevie hurried off. Carole and Cam had already disappeared somewhere, and the rest of the crowd had dissipated, too.

Lisa was relieved to have a moment to gather her thoughts. While she was happy that Red and Denise had decided to make a future together, she had mixed feelings about the whole topic of looking toward the future. *It'll be great to see them tie the knot,* she thought wistfully. *I just wish I knew whether I was still going to be living here when their baby is born.*

She was so deep in thought that it took her a moment to realize that the only other person left in the entryway with her was Scott Forester. He was watching her steadily, his blue eyes thoughtful but friendly.

Lisa gulped, suddenly feeling awkward. "Um, pretty big news, huh?" she said lamely.

"The biggest," Scott agreed. He took a few steps toward her, shoving both hands into the pockets of his khaki pants. "It was nice of Max to offer to throw them a wedding."

"That's Max for you." Lisa shrugged and smiled, thinking fondly of all the nice things the stable owner had done for so many people over the years, herself included. "He likes to act all gruff and stern and everything, but underneath it all he's just a big softy. Besides, Red has been working here since before I started riding. And Denise has been here for a long time, too. They're practically like family to him, you know?"

"Uh-huh. I guess Max treats all his staff like family," Scott commented. "So when the new stable hand gets here, should we say she's starting work or getting adopted?" He grinned, then shrugged apologetically for the lame joke. "She starts tomorrow, right?"

"I think so." Lisa had almost forgotten that Max's new hire was starting the next day. The stable owner had been looking for another hand to join Pine Hollow's small staff for some time, and he had finally found someone he liked. With a stab of guilt, Lisa realized that she didn't even know how Carole felt about that. After all, until her grounding Carole had been an important member of Max's staff.

Of course, Carole's not the only one adjusting to disturbing news these days, Lisa reminded herself with a twinge of self-pity. In addition to her new arrangement with Alex, her mother had recently announced—totally out of the blue, as far as Lisa was concerned—that she wanted to move to New Jersey to be closer to her sister, Marianne. Even days later, Lisa could hardly believe that her mother could really expect her to pack up and move to a new home, a new school, a whole new state, right in the middle of her senior year. Still, after her parents' sudden divorce, Lisa had learned that the unexpected really could happen.

Just about the only thing distracting her from worrying even more about where she was going to be living the next month was thinking about Scott. The previous Friday night the two of them had attended a party together, and much to her surprise, Lisa had had a great time with him. She'd been even more surprised at her reaction when he'd kissed her good night at the end of the evening. It felt disloyal to feel so strongly attracted to another guy so soon after breaking up with Alex, but she just couldn't help it. *And why shouldn't I be attracted to him?* she asked herself. *He's pretty damned attractive. Just ask any girl who's ever met him.* Sneaking a quick peek at Scott to confirm that opinion, she found him looking straight back at her with a slight smile on his handsome face.

Lisa gulped. Trying to cover her consternation by turning her head quickly and pretending to study the lucky horseshoe nailed to the wall near the door, she cleared her throat. "Um, I'd better head into the locker room and grab my riding gloves. If I don't take them home and wash them soon, they'll be ready to stand up and hit the trails on their own."

Scott chuckled and wandered after her as she headed into the student locker room. One wall of the large, square area was lined with roomy cubbies, where regular riders could stow their street clothes, schoolbooks, and other paraphernalia while they rode. Perching on the bench in front of her assigned cubby, Lisa leaned in and shoved aside a couple of sweatshirts and her spare jumping bat until she found the gloves she was seeking.

Wrinkling her nose at the caked-on dirt decorating the palms of both gloves, she realized she'd let her laundry duties go even longer than she'd thought. *Not that it matters,* she thought moodily. *If Mom goes through with these moving plans, I may not need riding gloves at all before long. Who knows if they even have decent stables in New Jersey?*

"So I was thinking. . . . If you're not doing

anything this weekend, maybe we could go grab some dinner."

"What?" Lisa was so caught up in her gloomy thoughts that she didn't really take in what Scott had said until about three seconds later. "Oh. Um, I don't know. I—I'll have to think about it."

Scott looked surprised. Was that a flash of hurt in his eyes? Lisa wasn't sure—it was gone almost before it appeared. "Okay," he said in his usual easy, casual tone. "No pressure. Let me know when the jury returns its verdict."

"All right." Lisa felt her cheeks turning pink. She was afraid she'd hurt his feelings, and that was the last thing she wanted to do. But she wasn't quite sure how to fix things now, especially since she really wasn't sure whether it was a good idea to go out with him again. "I'd better go. I told Stevie I'd help her haul wood for the Starlight Ride, and if I don't hop to it, she'll probably clobber me with a log." Smiling weakly, she turned and hurried out of the room, feeling Scott's gaze on her back but not quite daring to turn and see for sure.

Stevie flipped up the saddle flap and tightened the girth one notch on the saddle she'd just put on Senator, a dark bay Morgan gelding. She and her boyfriend, Phil, were going for a quick late-afternoon trail ride together at Cross County Stables, where Phil took lessons.

"There you go, bub," she told the horse cheerfully, dropping the leather flap and giving the horse a pat on the shoulder. Senator turned and glared at her suspiciously, his ears back and an annoyed expression on his long face. Stevie ignored it. She'd ridden the bay Morgan before, and she knew that his bad attitude would disappear as soon as she was in the saddle.

Humming under her breath, she reached for the bridle, automatically going through the motions of wrestling the reluctant gelding's head down low enough for her to slip the bit into his mouth. She was busy picturing how much fun she and Phil were going to have at Red and Denise's wedding. She'd told her boyfriend all about the double announcement as soon as she'd arrived at Cross County, and while Phil had pretended to moan and groan about having to wear a suit and tie on New Year's Eve, Stevie could tell that he was as excited as she was at suddenly having such romantic plans for the big night rather than just sitting around the Lakes' living room watching Dick Clark on TV and listening to Stevie's three brothers holding their annual New Year's Eve burping contest.

She was fastening the throatlatch of Senator's

bridle a moment later when she heard hoofbeats clip-clopping their way toward the Morgan's stall. "That you?" she called.

"Nope," Phil's familiar voice replied teasingly. "It's a total stranger. Ready to go?"

"In a sec." Stevie clenched her teeth as she tightened the girth another notch, smacking Senator soundly on the shoulder as he turned and nipped at the shoulder of her jacket. "Okay, now I'm ready."

Slipping Senator's reins over his head, she led him out of the stall and into the aisle, where Phil was waiting with his horse, Teddy. The Marstens lived just down the road from Cross County Stables, so Phil had ridden his affable gelding over to the stable rather than renting one of his instructor's school horses.

Outside, Stevie pulled down her stirrups and checked the girth one last time, then led Senator to the mounting block and swung into the saddle. As she waited for Phil to mount, her thoughts were already turning away from Red and Denise and back to more pressing issues. "So, Lisa and I just spent the last hour hauling wood," she said as Phil clucked to Teddy, bringing him up beside Stevie's horse. "While we worked we were talking about all the Starlight Rides we've been on, and she gave me some good ideas for my article."

"Really? Let's hear them," Phil said agreeably.

Stevie smiled as the two of them started off toward the trails. She loved talking about the work she was doing for the *Sentinel*. It was hard to believe that just a few weeks ago she'd never really even thought about becoming a reporter. "Well, I was thinking I might start out by describing how it feels to ride through the woods at night," she began.

By the time the two of them were leaning forward to help their horses climb the steep incline leading to one of their favorite trails, they had discussed the topic of Stevie's article thoroughly, and her thoughts were shifting gears once again. "Hey," she called to Phil, who was slightly ahead of her on the wide trail. "Have you seen much of A.J. this weekend?"

Phil glanced at her over his shoulder, then pulled back his horse as they reached the top of the hill to let Stevie come abreast of him. "Not much," he said. "I think he's working on some kind of take-home test for English class."

"I wonder if he's going to try to track down that woman." Stevie was trying to sound casual, but she was brimming with curiosity. Phil's best friend, A.J. McDonnell, had recently discovered that his parents had adopted him as a baby and never told him about it. He hadn't dealt with the revelation very well at first—he'd more or less stopped talking to his family and friends, started skipping school and failing tests, and even developed the beginnings of a

29

drinking problem before finally realizing that he was only hurting himself. The previous week, while looking through old issues of the local newspaper as part of a research project, Stevie had found a photograph of a woman who looked so much like A.J. that Stevie was certain she had to be his birth mother. What would A.J. do with the information? Stevie had no idea. But she thought that if he didn't do something soon, she just might burst.

Phil shot her a look that said he knew exactly what she was thinking. "I don't know," he said. "And I don't think we should hassle him about it. It's up to him now. If he decides he doesn't want to deal, we have to be his friends and respect that."

Stevie sighed, knowing he was right but hating to admit it. She wasn't A.J., and A.J. wasn't her. As much as she wanted him to track down that woman—his mother?—it had to be his decision. "Yeah, yeah," she muttered. "I guess he has to make up his own mind and all that. I just wish he'd hurry up about it."

"Yeah, me too," Phil admitted with a wry grin. "He still isn't saying too much about what's going on in his head, but I just keep thinking how hard this must be. Especially now with the whole family holiday thing going on all around him."

Stevie nodded, trying to imagine what it would be like to be in A.J.'s shoes. Finally she shook her head, deciding it was just too far outside of anything she knew. "So, speaking of the holidays," she said, deciding it was time for a lighter subject, "I was planning to get you your usual lump of coal for Christmas. And eight smaller lumps for Hanukkah. What do you think?"

Phil grinned. He was half Christian and half Jewish, so he liked to tease Stevie by acting disgruntled when she only got him a single gift rather than one for each holiday. "Sure," he said. "As long as you're okay with your usual gift of a half-eaten jelly doughnut."

Stevie stuck out her tongue at him. But their joking around had reminded her of something. Christmas was only ten days away, and with all the excitement of joining the *Sentinel*, working on the Starlight Ride, riding in a prestigious horse show the previous month, and everything else that had been going on in her life, Stevie hadn't found much time for holiday shopping. She'd managed to pick up Christmas gifts for Carole and Lisa—they were pretty easy to shop for—but so far she hadn't come across anything that seemed just right for Phil. "So," she said, deciding it was as good a time as any to start fishing for gift ideas. "What kind of loot are you expecting from the folks this year?"

Phil shrugged as he guided his horse around a large pinecone on the trail, which Teddy was eyeing as suspiciously as if it were some kind of deadly horse-eating monster. "Not sure," he said. "I asked Mom and Dad for a new close-contact saddle, but I don't know if they're going to go for it. Dad will probably have a heart attack when he finds out what they cost."

Stevie grinned. Her parents had bought her a dressage saddle the previous Christmas, and she still remembered her brothers' howls of disbelief when they'd found out how much it cost. "I know what you mean. Alex, Chad, and Michael claim they're not getting me Christmas presents ever again after last year. Some sort of protest thing."

"My sisters will probably just chip in and buy me some lame sweater like they usually do." Phil rolled his eyes. "Maybe I can exchange it for a couple of pairs of jeans. I've been riding so much lately that I've practically worn holes in the legs of all the ones I already have."

He laughed, and Stevie chuckled along, but inside her head, little bells were going off. *Was that a hint?* she wondered. The first thing that had popped into her mind when Phil had made the comment was the absolutely gorgeous pair of top-grain leather schooling chaps she'd seen in The Saddlery recently. *It had to be a hint. Phil only has that one pair of grungy old half chaps. He's probably dying for a really nice pair of full-length ones.*

"What about you?" Phil asked after a moment, shooting Stevie a meaningful look. "Is there anything in particular that you're craving for Christmas this year? You get extra points if it's something that a well-meaning but shopping-impaired boyfriend could pick up without fighting the crowds at the mall."

"Hmmm?" Stevie hardly took in the question. She was too busy trying to remember the price of those chaps. "Oh, I don't know. Maybe something small, like a nice trip to Florida for me and Belle," she joked absentmindedly. "The stable's been kind of cool lately, and Max absolutely refuses to put a little furnace in Belle's stall for those crisp winter mornings when things get frosty. If the weather gets much colder, Belle's going to start insisting on wearing a blanket in her stall instead of just for turnout."

She realized she was babbling randomly, but fortunately Phil didn't seem to mind. Stevie didn't want him to realize that her mind was working overtime as she chattered on and on about the weather, trying to figure out the quickest and easiest ways to pick up a few extra bucks before Christmas.

It's not going to be easy to come up with that kind of money in the next week, especially when I already have so much to do, like writing my article and helping with the Starlight Ride. Not to mention minor stuff like school and sleep. She glanced over at her boyfriend, remembering the way the smooth, buttery leather of those chaps had felt beneath her fingers. She could already picture the look of amazement and adoration that would cross his face when he opened the box. *But Phil is worth it. If it's chaps he wants, it's chaps he's going to get!*

THREE

Lisa blinked in surprise as she snapped out of her thoughts long enough to notice that she was about to drive right past Pine Hollow's driveway. She was slightly amazed, as always, at the way she could be thinking about something else entirely while she drove, yet find herself going through the automatic motions of putting the key in the ignition, shifting into gear, and all the other little actions that were involved in driving. It was sort of like the way things had come together when she got good at riding. When she was first learning, she had been sure she'd never be able to remember everything that went into it—keeping her heels down and her elbows in, holding the reins correctly, coordinating her aids. Driving a car wasn't quite as complicated as riding a horse, but it was still pretty impressive that she could drive all the way from Willow Creek High School to Pine Hollow without paying the slightest bit of attention to what she was doing. *I guess it's because the route is so familiar,* she thought as she tapped the brake to slow down for the turn. *I'm sure things will be very different if we move to New Jersey next month. I'll need to learn a whole new route to a whole new school. From a whole new house. And I'll have to make all new friends. . . .*

She grimaced, shaking her head as if the action could shake the whole moving plan out of existence. It was impossible, that was all. There was no way she could pick up her whole life and start over right in the middle of her senior year. No way her mother could expect that of her, no matter how miserable her own life might be these days. Lisa would just have to make her mother see that.

Easier said than done, she thought grimly, pulling into the small gravel parking area across the yard from the stable building. *Once Mom makes up her mind about something, she can be harder to convince than a mule with an attitude problem.*

Cutting the ignition, Lisa sighed. She would just have to find a way, that was all. The logical first step would be talking to her friends about it. She was at Pine Hollow to meet Stevie and Carole for an after-school trail ride. Ever since they'd first met and become best friends, the three of them had helped each other out of more jams than Lisa could count. She knew she could rely on them to do whatever they could to help her now.

I just hope Carole doesn't bring Cam along today.

The thought slipped out before Lisa knew it was coming. She winced, feeling like a jerk, but she couldn't quite take back the sentiment. She had always liked Carole's boyfriend, Cam Nelson—he had lived in Virginia back when they were all in junior high, though his family had moved to Los Angeles before Lisa had really gotten to know him. But his sudden reappearance—and the way he and Carole had become inseparable virtually overnight—had left her a little off-balance.

Lisa was happy for Carole, of course. It was nice to see her friend getting some long-overdue male attention. But that didn't make it any easier to watch Carole and Cam eagerly flinging themselves into the early stages of falling in love, especially when all of it reminded Lisa of the days when she and Alex couldn't keep their hands off each other when they were together and couldn't go more than five minutes without mentioning each other's names when they were apart.

But that wasn't the only reason she hoped Cam wouldn't tag along that day. Sometimes it was really nice to hang out with her friends when it was just the three of them, like in the old days when they'd spent so much time together—mostly at the stable—that they'd dubbed themselves The Saddle Club.

Thinking about the past was making Lisa feel gloomy, so she did her best to push those thoughts aside as she headed toward the stable entrance. It was sunny and fairly warm for December, so the big double doors were standing open. As she reached them, she saw that Max was just inside, talking to a tall, rail-thin young woman with wavy dark hair pulled into a high ponytail.

Lisa hesitated at the entrance, not wanting to barge in on a meeting with a new student or boarder. But Max spotted her and waved her over. "Lisa!" he exclaimed in his most jovial tone. "Come on over here. I want you to meet someone."

Lisa was surprised. Pine Hollow had been busier than ever lately—there was a lot of development going on in the area, and it seemed that every new family that moved to town had at least one member who wanted to take riding lessons. Max always worked hard, but in the past few months he'd been run ragged. Lisa couldn't remember the last time she'd seen him so happy and relaxed.

Glancing at the strange woman curiously, she waited for Max to introduce them. It didn't take long.

"Lisa Atwood is one of our longtime riders," he told the newcomer, patting Lisa on the back. "And Lisa, this is the new stable hand I mentioned the other day. Maureen Chance. Today's her first day on the job."

"Oh! Hello." Lisa realized she should have guessed the young woman's identity right away. "Nice to meet you, Maureen."

"Likewise," Maureen replied. Her voice was surprisingly deep for her appearance and age—sort of husky and raw, a voice one might expect from a country-and-western singer. "You're not the kid whose job I took, are you?"

Lisa blinked, startled by the new stable hand's bluntness. "Uh, no," she said. "That's my friend Carole. My best friend." She wasn't sure why Maureen's comment made her feel defensive, but she couldn't help feeling a little put off by it. "She's meeting me here today, actually."

Maureen shrugged. "Guess I'll meet her soon, then," she said easily.

"Actually, I should have been clearer about Carole," Max said, shooting Lisa a cautious glance. "As I mentioned, she recently had to, uh, take a break from her job here. But you're not exactly replacing her. I needed more help anyway, so when Carole's ready, I hope she'll be back to work right alongside you and the others."

Maureen nodded politely, though Lisa couldn't help thinking that she didn't seem very interested in

Max's explanation. *I don't know what I was expecting the new stable hand to be like,* Lisa thought. *But whatever I might have imagined, Maureen definitely isn't it.*

As Maureen turned away to ask Max something about her work schedule, Lisa furtively gave her a once-over. She was pretty in an angular sort of way, with long legs, a wide smile, and eyes that were an interesting shade of medium brown, flecked with green and gold. She appeared to be somewhere in her early to mid-twenties.

As Lisa was staring thoughtfully at the small horseshoe tattoo on the newcomer's collarbone, Maureen glanced over and caught her gaze. Lisa blushed and averted her eyes quickly, while Maureen laughed. "Don't worry, I don't care if you want to check me out," she said, shooting Max a wink and a grin before turning her almost disturbingly direct gaze back to Lisa. "I know I'm the new kid in town, so it's only natural y'all will be curious. You can even ask me questions if you want to. And if you're lucky, I just might tell you the truth when I answer 'em."

Lisa had no idea how to respond to that. Pulling up every ounce of the good manners her mother had drilled into her at an early age, she cleared her throat. "Actually, I was just wondering where you worked before this."

"Well, I just moved up here from Norfolk, and I worked at a stable down there for a couple of years. Before that . . ."

There was more, but Lisa didn't really take it in. She just nodded along politely, pretending to listen to the details and wondering how, after meeting her only minutes earlier, she could already be so certain that she wasn't going to like Maureen Chance much at all.

Carole was thinking about Cam as she stuck her car keys in her jacket pocket and hurried toward Pine Hollow's main entrance. *I wish he could have come along today instead of going to that team meeting,* she thought wistfully. *Especially since he's leaving town next week. With everything that's going on, we might not have much chance to see each other before then.* She was looking forward to riding with her friends, of course, but she couldn't help thinking that she would be looking forward to it even more if her boyfriend were going to be there, too.

As she stepped through the door, she stopped short in surprise. Lisa was standing in the entryway, talking to someone—a woman about Denise's age, dressed in jeans and well-worn rubber muckers. Max was standing nearby, beaming contentedly. As soon as she saw the stranger, Carole knew who she had to be: the new stable hand.

41

Lisa spotted Carole almost immediately. "Hi!" she called, waving. "Come here and meet Maureen. Maureen Chance. She's the new stable hand."

Carole forced a welcoming smile onto her face, though it felt stiff and unwieldy there, like the fake plastic clown lips she'd once worn with a childhood Halloween costume. "Hi, Maureen," she said, stepping forward to join the others. "I'm Carole Hanson. Um, I used to work here."

"So I hear." Maureen looked her up and down curiously.

Carole shifted her weight from one foot to the other, suddenly feeling like a bug pinned to a card in a museum exhibit. "Uh, so it's your first day, huh?"

Before Maureen could answer, Sarah Anne Porter, a sixth-grade rider, rushed out of the stable aisle and skidded to a stop in the entryway. "Max!" she exclaimed breathlessly. "It's Comanche. He keeps trying to bite me when I groom him."

Max frowned. "First of all, what have I told you about running in the stable?"

"Sorry," Sarah Anne said sheepishly, blushing slightly. "But what should I do? I think he hates me."

Carole opened her mouth to reassure the younger girl, but Maureen beat her to it. "Don't sweat it, kid," she told Sarah Anne. "I'm sure he's just seeing what he can get away with. He can tell you're scared of him, so he's acting like a brat. Come on, and I'll show that old nag who's boss for you."

"Thanks, Maureen." Max beamed as if the new stable hand had just offered to single-handedly tame a whole herd of mustangs, rather than just discipline a generally placid school horse. "Go on now, Sarah Anne. Maureen will help you. You pay attention to what she tells you, okay?"

"Okay." The younger rider shot the new stable hand an inquisitive look, then followed obediently as Maureen led the way back toward the stable aisle, her stride long and fast.

Max blinked at Carole and Lisa. "So what are you two up to today? And where's the third musketeer?"

Carole was so busy trying to act normal—to keep herself from revealing how weird she felt about the fact that a total stranger was there, doing the job that should have been hers—that for a second she had no idea what Max was talking about. Fortunately, Lisa answered for both of them.

"I don't know where Stevie is." Lisa checked her watch. "She was supposed to meet us here for a trail ride."

As if on cue, Stevie burst into the stable, breathless from hurrying. "Sorry I'm late," she gasped. "I had to walk. My inconsiderate dolt of a brother took off with the car again."

"Okay, I'll leave you to it, then," Max said, turning and heading toward the office.

Stevie waved. "Nice chatting with you, Max!" she called teasingly. Then she glanced at her friends. "Ready to go? Hey, what's with you two? You look weird."

"We just met the new stable hand," Lisa said.

Carole nodded slowly, hoping that her friends couldn't tell how freaked out she was. *It's stupid to feel so threatened by someone you just met*, she told herself sternly. *It's no big deal. Pine Hollow's getting busier all the time, and Max needs more help. That's all. It has nothing to do with you.*

Stevie's eyes widened. "Really? So what's she like?"

"She seems to know what she's doing, I guess," Lisa replied blandly. "You'll probably meet her before long. Come on, should we hit the trail?"

Stevie shrugged agreeably, and Carole puffed out her cheeks with relief. She knew that her friends would be supportive, no matter what she was feeling. But she still didn't want to spend too much time discussing the new stable hand just then.

As Lisa hurried off to check the lessons list posted in the locker room to see which horse was free for her to use, Carole and Stevie headed toward the tack room. Stevie was chattering about her latest newspaper article, but Carole wasn't really listening. She was too busy trying to convince herself that it was no big deal that someone new would be working at Pine Hollow.

It's not like Max hasn't told me a million times that there will always be a job for me here, she reminded herself as she stood on tiptoes to grab Starlight's bridle from its usual hook in the tack room. *I'm sure Dad will let me start working again after the holidays, and then everything will go back to normal.*

But even as she thought it, she knew it probably wasn't going to happen. Too much had changed lately for things ever to be quite like they were before. Some of the changes were good ones—her relationship with Cam, for instance. Others were definitely bad, like being grounded and having to quit her job, not to mention having to earn back her father's trust after the cheating incident. And then there were the changes that were just plain confusing. Like the way she and Ben Marlow had seemed to be getting closer before Cam had come back into her life, and how she still felt her stomach flip over nervously whenever she saw Ben—even though she and Cam were in love now, and even though she still had no idea if Ben had ever felt anything special for her anyway. And the way Carole's father kept talking about all the prestigious colleges he wanted her to attend, ever since she had received her surprisingly high PSAT scores a few weeks earlier. And now there was Maureen Chance to add to the perplexing parade of changes that her life had become.

I don't know why this has to be so hard, she thought, frustrated at her inability to make sense of it all. *All I want to do is survive high school, then spend the rest of my life working with horses. What's so complicated about that?*

But she knew better. How could she expect things to be simple when she couldn't even figure out exactly what she wanted to do after high school? For as long as she could remember, she had been saying that she wanted to work with horses full-time someday. But what did that mean, really? As far as she could tell, it meant giving up parts of what she loved so that she could focus on other parts. If she decided to be a competitive rider, it meant there probably wouldn't be much time for stuff like working with a wide variety of horses or teaching beginning riders to love the sport as much as she did. On the other hand, if she followed in Max's footsteps and built up her own lessons stable, it would almost certainly mean giving up any lingering dreams of gold hunt cups or Olympic stardom.

Of course, if Dad has his way, I'll have plenty of time to figure it out while I rot away in some liberal arts classroom at some snooty university, Carole thought ruefully. *I don't want to disappoint him. But why can't he realize that that sort of thing just isn't for me?*

Carole was still pondering her uncertain future twenty minutes later as she and her friends set off across the fields on their horses. Lisa was riding a school horse named Checkers, Carole was mounted on Starlight, and Stevie was aboard her spirited Arabian-Saddlebred mare, Belle.

As the three girls approached the edge of the woods beyond Pine Hollow's big south pasture, Carole suddenly realized that she'd hardly heard a word either of her friends had said since they'd set out. Feeling guilty, she racked her brain, trying to remember any of the conversation. But all she could recall hearing was a lot of discussion about Stevie's newspaper article. At the moment, they seemed to be talking about A.J. and his adoption problems.

Okay, it's way past time to drag yourself out of this gutter of pathetic self-involvement and start thinking about something else, she told herself firmly as she shortened Starlight's stride to keep him from running up on Checkers. *Like Cam, for instance.*

Even the thought of his name made her smile. Once again, she wished that he had been able to join them that day. It was hard to accept that they wouldn't be seeing that much of each other for most of the next couple of weeks. At least she could look forward to their special get-together on New Year's

Eve. Thinking about that reminded her that she still hadn't come up with any brilliant ideas about what to get him for Christmas.

"Hey, you guys," she blurted out, interrupting something Stevie was saying about A.J.'s parents. "I just realized I need to start shopping for a Christmas present for Cam. What do you think I should get him?"

Stevie seemed startled by the sudden change in topic, but she shrugged good-naturedly as she brought Belle to a halt and glanced over at Carole. "I don't know," she said, leaning forward to give her mare a pat on the withers. "But listen, that reminds me. I finally figured out the perfect gift for Phil!"

"What is it?" Carole asked, hoping she could pick up some hints from Stevie's gift idea. Cam and Phil didn't know each other too well—maybe Carole could even get the same thing her friend was getting for her boyfriend, just to play it safe. She was sure Stevie wouldn't mind.

Stevie grinned, looking pleased with herself. "I got the idea yesterday when he kept complaining about how all his jeans are, like, worn through from riding so much. He might as well have just come right out and said, 'Stevie, please please please would you buy me those gorgeous leather schooling chaps in the window display at The Saddlery?'

Luckily I could tell that was what he was thinking. So that's what I'm getting him."

"Really?" Lisa sounded surprised. "Wow. I've seen those chaps. That's a pretty extravagant gift."

Carole bit her lip, staring down at Starlight's glossy mahogany neck without really seeing it. She knew exactly which chaps Stevie meant—she too had seen them the last time she'd been at the mall, and they really were pretty spectacular. "I think it sounds like a really romantic gift. I'm sure Phil will love them. Um . . ." She hesitated. "Do you mind if I ask how much they cost?"

Stevie shrugged. "Why would I mind? It's not like you couldn't just walk into the store yourself and find out anyway." She grinned, then told them the price.

Carole gasped at the amount, dismayed at how much Stevie was planning to spend. Was that the sort of money she would be expected to shell out now that she and Cam were a couple?

Probably not, she thought uncertainly, hiding her consternation from her friends by leaning over to fiddle with her stirrup. *After all, Stevie and Phil have been together for years. Cam and I have been a couple for only a short time. It's not like he's going to expect anything that generous from me. Is he?*

As she straightened up in the saddle again, Lisa

shot her a shrewd glance. "Don't worry, Carole," she said. "Just because Stevie's suddenly turned into Ms. High Roller, it doesn't mean you have to mortgage Starlight to buy Cam a Christmas present. It's the thought that counts, remember?"

"Definitely," Stevie agreed. "He'll be thrilled with anything you pick out, Carole. Especially if you wear something really hot when you give it to him." She batted her eyelashes playfully.

Carole blushed. "Um, so how are you going to afford those chaps, anyway?" she asked Stevie. "Last I heard, you were so broke you were borrowing money from your brothers to pay your library fines."

"Good point," Stevie said. "And I must admit, at first I thought that might be a problem myself. But then I had another brilliant idea. I'm planning to ask all three of my brothers to give me cash this year instead of buying me presents." She adjusted her riding helmet and grinned at her friends proudly. "They always leave their shopping until the last minute anyway, then spend half of Christmas moaning and groaning and complaining about how hard I am to shop for. I'm sure they'll be thrilled that I'm letting them off the hook."

Carole nodded. Knowing Stevie's brothers, that was probably true. Still, she was impressed that Stevie was planning to lay out so much cash for one

Christmas present. *Wow,* she thought. *Am I going to have to start buying Starlight the economy brand of horse treats so that I can afford to have a boyfriend?*

She realized she was being silly. For one thing, she was sure that Cam wouldn't want her to bankrupt herself or deprive her horse for his sake. He cared about her, and that was way more important than any Christmas gift. Still, it was just one more thing to worry about.

Stevie and Lisa had already switched topics and were discussing which trail to take, but Carole couldn't seem to focus on what her friends were saying. *This is our first Christmas together, and I want it to be perfect,* she thought as she stared blankly over Starlight's head into the trees beyond. *That means I need to figure out the perfect gift for Cam. And I don't have much time.*

FOUR

"So what do you think is wrong with George?" Scott asked Callie as he merged onto Highway 12.

Callie chewed on her lower lip and shook her head. She'd been asking herself that same question all weekend, though not in the way Scott meant it. George had been out sick that day at school, which meant that Callie hadn't seen him since Friday, the day after their big confrontation. "I don't know, and to be honest, I don't much care," she told her brother, tapping nervously on the door handle. "All I care about is whether he realizes I was serious about what I told him the other day. I just hope he got the hint this time."

Scott turned his attention away from the road just long enough to shoot her a reassuring smile. "I'm sure he did," he said. "You can be pretty clear when you want to be."

"Don't remind me," Callie muttered, sinking

down slightly in her seat as she remembered yelling at George, telling him in no uncertain terms that their friendship was over. She still felt a twinge of guilt whenever she thought about it. How had an acquaintance that had started so casually gotten so out of control? She still wondered if there was something she could have done differently—maybe been more firm about his behavior from the start or asked one of her friends to talk to him. It wasn't that she particularly valued George's friendship for its own sake, but she felt bad about possibly hurting such an insecure and seemingly lonely soul. George didn't seem to have many close friends aside from his horse, a lovely Trakehner mare named Joyride. Even now, after all the trouble he'd been, Callie felt sorry for him.

With a determined effort, she pushed aside all thoughts of George as she climbed out of the car. He had ruined her first visit with this particular horse; there was no way she was going to let it happen again.

A tall, thin man was strolling toward them, a welcoming smile on his tanned, heavily lined face. "Howdy again, folks," he called in a soft Virginia drawl. "Welcome back." He gestured toward a nearby paddock, where a leopard-spot Appaloosa gelding was tied to a rail. "Scooby's over there if you want to get right to it."

"Sounds good," Scott replied, extending his hand to the farm owner. "Nice to see you again, Mr. Rayburn. Thanks for letting us come out for another look."

Callie added her thanks, then followed her brother and Mr. Rayburn over to the paddock. She had already decided to be honest with Scooby's owner. "I'm afraid I was a little distracted the last time I came out," she told him apologetically. "It might be best if we could just sort of start all over again."

The man looked a little surprised, but he nodded agreeably. "All right, then," he said amiably. "Then allow me to introduce you to Scooby." He reached over the fence to pat the horse on the neck. Scooby didn't respond; he merely flicked his tail at a fly.

Callie gave Scooby a few pats and scratches to get reacquainted, then stepped back so that Mr. Rayburn could put the horse through his paces. As he did, he chatted easily about the horse's quirks and temperament.

"What do you think?" Scott asked Callie in a low voice as the farm owner jogged along, leading the Appaloosa at a trot. "Was it worth a second trip?"

"We'll see," Callie muttered, never taking her gaze off the horse. Scooby definitely had the build for endurance riding—rangy, straight-legged, and symmetrical, somewhere just over fifteen hands by her estimate. His nostrils were large, his shoulders sloped nicely, and his hindquarters showed good definition.

She watched carefully as Mr. Rayburn led the horse around the paddock, first at a walk and then at a trot. Scooby moved well, his hooves skimming the ground as he moved. *Nice, efficient movement,* Callie thought, checking off another box on her mental list of things to watch for in evaluating the horse.

Finally Mr. Rayburn brought Scooby back to a walk, giving him a fond pat on the neck before leading him toward the fence. "There you go," he told Callie, a little breathless from exertion, though Scooby hadn't turned a hair. "One thing I forgot to mention on your last visit. He's not wearing shoes right now—never really needed 'em, with his feet. So you would need to talk to your farrier about how best to handle that."

Callie nodded, pleased to hear that the gelding was able to go barefoot. Good, solid feet were important in any horse, but in an endurance prospect they were paramount. Scooby really didn't seem to have any major flaws, at least not in his conformation, balance, or movement. The only thing that concerned her a little was whether the horse had the right attitude for her. So far he appeared to be pretty calm and quiet—a good temperament for an endurance horse, which can't afford to use up a lot of energy on nerves or bad behavior. But Callie knew she wouldn't be happy with a horse that was *too* sedate. She liked a mental challenge when she was riding and had always sought out horses that would never let her get too comfortable—or bored.

There's only one way to find out, she thought.

As if reading her mind, Mr. Rayburn held out the reins. "Want to give him a whirl?"

"Thanks." Callie took the reins and looped them back over Scooby's head. Not bothering to use the fence to mount, she grabbed a handful of mane and sprang into the saddle.

As soon as she settled into position, she knew that, despite his calm outer appearance, Scooby wasn't lazy or a pushover. She could feel him responding from the moment she began communicating with him; she could sense his mind working beneath his pricked ears.

Wow, Callie thought. *What a difference from Barq. Like night and day.*

She stayed in the saddle for a good long time, testing Scooby in every way she could devise to make sure that her first impression hadn't been wrong. He didn't let her down. By the time she swung out of the saddle, she was more pleased than ever with the horse. He wasn't perfect—she could already tell that he needed some conditioning, and his suppling needed a little fine-tuning. But riding him after her weeks of struggling with Barq was like diving into a cool, inviting pool after staggering out of a desert.

She was careful to keep her enthusiasm out of her face and voice as she led Scooby back toward Mr. Rayburn and Scott. She loosened the gelding's girth and fiddled with his head and ears for a moment, making sure he wouldn't give her any trouble on the ground. "He feels pretty good," she said casually, finally giving the horse a pat and turning to face his owner. "I'll have to think about it some more. What are you asking for him?"

Mr. Rayburn named a figure. Callie nearly gasped in shock—not because the amount was too much, but because it was so much less than the price of most of the other horses she'd seen during her search.

It's almost too good to be true, she thought as she and Scott said good-bye and headed back to the car.

"So? What did you think?" Scott asked as he started the engine a moment later.

"I think he felt pretty good," Callie said cautiously, unwilling to go on record with her true thoughts just yet. She certainly didn't want to rush this decision—not after waiting so long to get here. "Definitely a contender. We'll see."

Scott nodded, seeming satisfied with that. As he

put the car in gear and pulled out of the parking area, he glanced over at her. "By the way, I was thinking about something while you were riding," he said seriously. "If you think it'll help, I could talk to George for you tomorrow. You know—just make sure there's no misunderstanding or anything."

"What? Oh, that's okay." Callie waved one hand to brush away the mention of George's name. He was the last thing she wanted to think about. Thanks to Scooby the wonder horse, she had much better things to occupy her mind.

"Back inside, boy," Carole told Starlight as she led him into his stall. "Sorry you couldn't hang out with your friends a little longer. I would've liked to hang around with my friends a little longer, too."

She shook her head, not wanting to slip into self-pity again. She would have loved to stay out with Stevie and Lisa, who had decided to take advantage of the lingering afternoon sunshine by walking their horses around the back paddock for a while, even though they had cooled them down sufficiently on the way back across the fields. Carole guessed that they just wanted a chance to spend more time discussing the Starlight Ride and A.J.'s problems and Maureen Chance and all the other topics that Carole had barely paid attention to during their ride. But because of her curfew, she didn't have time to hang out. Her father had been awfully nice to allow her to start riding again before her punishment was technically over, and Carole didn't want to give him cause to regret it. As hard as it was to leave the stable after only a couple of hours, it would be harder still to be banned again.

Slipping Starlight's halter on, she quickly looped his lead rope through the ring mounted on the stall wall. Maybe she didn't have time to shoot the breeze with her friends, but at least she could spend a few minutes giving her horse a decent grooming. After unbuckling the girth, she pulled the saddle off his back and slung it over the half door. Then she checked her watch.

"Damn," she muttered. It was later than she'd thought. There wouldn't be enough time for a leisurely grooming that day after all.

Still, she couldn't leave without giving Starlight at least a cursory brushing. She grabbed her grooming kit and set to work.

She was running the body brush over his left foreleg when she felt the soft bristles catch on something. "What's that?" she murmured, tucking the brush under her arm and leaning in closer to run her hands over the spot. She was expecting to find a burr stuck in the hair, but instead her gently prodding fingers discovered a small abrasion on the pastern. "Uh-oh," she told her horse, standing up and giving

59

him a pat. "Looks like you scraped yourself on something out there."

While any injury to a horse's leg required attention, Carole wasn't too worried about what she was seeing. The scrape was clearly minor, and it didn't seem to be bothering the horse at all. Still, she made a mental note to mention it to Max so that he could have Judy Barker, the equine vet who looked after Pine Hollow's horses, take a quick look at it the next time she came by.

"I'll be right back, boy," she told Starlight, heading for the aisle. "I'm just going to get some antiseptic to put on that."

Carole could feel the minutes ticking away as she hurried toward the tack room. What was it about horses that made them always turn up lame or injured or colicky at the least convenient time imaginable? Now she was really going to have to hurry if she didn't want to be late.

The tack room was unoccupied when she entered, and she headed straight for the first-aid cabinet above the sink in the corner. Yanking it open, she spotted the bottle immediately. She grabbed it, standing on tiptoes to reach it on its high shelf. She realized a split second too late that someone hadn't bothered to wipe off the side of the bottle after pouring, and it was slippery. She fumbled for a grip, but it was no good. The thick glass bottle shot out

60

of her hands and arced toward the wall, hitting it with a solid crack.

Carole winced as the bottle fell to the floor in several pieces, its contents splattering everywhere. "Oh, great!" she cried in frustration, checking her watch again. Now she would have to spend valuable minutes cleaning up the mess, not to mention going all the way out to the equipment shed to get another bottle.

She spun around and grabbed for a paper towel. But only half a sheet came off in her hand. The roll was empty.

"Damn, damn, damn!" she cried. Then she remembered that Max kept surplus paper goods in the equipment shed. She would just have to grab another roll of paper towels when she went out there to get the ointment. Sighing heavily, she kicked the bottle pieces toward the wall so that no one would step on them, then spun around and hurried toward the back door.

The equipment shed was a multipurpose outbuilding where Max kept a variety of things, including the stable's tractor and harrow and some others pieces of large machinery and garden supplies. There was a separate section off to one side that consisted of floor-to-ceiling shelves packed with every conceivable item that a stable might need, from extra rolls of paper towels and toilet paper to spare bandages and medications, a bucketful of dusty riding crops, and miscellaneous farrier supplies.

As Carole pushed open the small building's wooden door and reached for the light switch just inside, she stopped short. The overhead bulb was already on. And lounging on the seat of the tractor, her long, lean legs propped up on the steering wheel and her flannel shirt half open, was the new stable hand, Maureen Chance. But it wasn't the young woman's partially visible tank top or her relaxed position that caught Carole's eye. It was the lit cigarette in her right hand.

Carole gasped. "What are you doing?" she cried. "Are you—are you *smoking*?"

"Uh-oh. Looks like I'm busted." Maureen grinned and tapped the cigarette on the side of the tractor seat, scattering ashes on the cement floor. "You better not rat me out to the teacher or I'll beat you up during recess."

Carole frowned. Maureen could kid around all she wanted to, but this was no joking matter. "Maybe Max didn't tell you," she said carefully, not wanting to pick a fight with the new hand on her first day. "He doesn't like people smoking in the stable."

Maureen shrugged and took a long drag. "We're not in the stable," she said, letting the smoke out in a puff and then glancing around at the walls of the shed, her eyebrow raised in an exaggerated query. "Are we?"

Carole's frown deepened as she wondered how to respond. Everyone knew that fire and stables weren't a good combination. If Maureen really had to smoke at all, Carole would have preferred to see her doing it out in the open, say in the middle of the schooling ring, where the only thing that might possibly catch fire was a jump or two, rather than here in the overstuffed equipment shed, where there were all kinds of flammable items that would smolder and burn without anyone even noticing until it was too late.

She was about to try to put some of that into words when she heard heavy footsteps approaching from outside. A moment later George Wheeler appeared in the doorway, an empty bucket in one hand.

"Oh." George looked sheepish as he skidded to a stop. "Sorry, didn't mean to interrupt. I didn't know anyone was out here."

Maureen lowered her cigarette and looked at him with interest. "Well, well, well," she drawled. "So there *are* a few actual guys around this place after all. I was starting to feel like I'd sailed away to the land of the Amazons. What's your name, big guy? I'm Maureen."

George blinked, gaping at Maureen as if she were

some strange new species that had just landed on earth. Carole ignored him as he stammered incoherently in response to Maureen's greeting. Her attention was fixed on the orange ember at the end of the stable hand's cigarette. One stray spark from it could spread into an inferno in a matter of seconds if the wind happened to be blowing the wrong way. Didn't Maureen realize that? How could she put the whole stable at risk for a lousy smoke?

"Uh, I'm George," George managed to choke out at last. "George Wheeler."

"Ah! I've seen your name somewhere." Maureen dragged thoughtfully on her cigarette. "You own that gorgeous chestnut mare with the blaze, right? The one in the stall next to Patch?"

"Right!" George said with obvious delight. "Her name's Joyride, but I usually just call her Joy."

Carole opened her mouth to interrupt the inane conversation and remind everyone that stable rules usually existed for a reason and the one about not smoking was particularly important. But before she could speak, she heard someone clearing his throat behind her. Glancing over her shoulder, she froze. Ben Marlow was standing behind George, looking from one of them to the other, a confused and slightly wary expression in his dark eyes.

"Ben!" Carole blurted out. "What are you doing here?"

She blushed wildly as she realized the lameness of her question, though Ben didn't seem to notice. He shrugged and gestured toward the supply shelves. "Paper towels," he said succinctly. "Someone made a real mess of the tack room."

"Oops. Uh, that was me." Carole blushed deeper than before, hardly noticing as George grabbed a bucket, slipped past her and exited without another word to any of them. "I just came out to get more paper towels myself, and then I was going to clean it up."

Meanwhile, Maureen was still puffing away, surveying them both from her position atop the tractor seat. "Good cover story, Ben," she commented with a laugh. "Now she'll never guess that you were really sneaking out here to meet me. Our little secret is still safe."

Ben shot Maureen a look Carole couldn't quite read. Without responding to the older stable hand's flirtation, he stepped around Carole and grabbed a roll of paper towels from the shelf beside her. "I'll clean up," he said. "Don't worry about it."

"Thanks." Carole could only assume that he was addressing her, since he hadn't bothered to look her way. "Thanks a lot, Ben." She found herself wanting to say something more—to keep him in the shed for at least a little while longer. But the right words evaded her, so all she could do was watch while he strode toward the door. Why did she have such a strong urge to hurry after him, to grab him by the arm and make him stay with her?

It's only natural, she told herself uncertainly. *He's your friend, and you haven't seen much of him lately, so I guess you must miss him. Miss him as a friend, that is. Nothing more than that.*

"Catch you later, hot stuff," Maureen called after him. Only a slight stiffening of Ben's back showed that he'd heard her.

Carole wrinkled her nose, realizing belatedly that Maureen was flirting with Ben in a big way. *Gross!* she thought. *She must be, like, five years older than him at least. Besides, Ben would never in a million years be interested in someone like her. She's so loud, so crude. Not to mention kind of obnoxious . . .*

She shook her head, wondering what Max had been thinking when he'd decided to hire Maureen Chance. Had he been so desperate to find someone to fill the position that he'd lowered his standards? Was it all Carole's fault for getting banned from her job just when things were the busiest?

Then again, maybe I'm just taking out my own feelings on Maureen, she thought. *I'm afraid of being replaced, so I'm looking for things to criticize about the new person. For all I know, Max told Maureen she could smoke in here.*

That last part didn't seem too likely, but how

could Carole know for sure? She didn't even work there anymore.

"That Ben's kind of a muffin, isn't he?" Maureen said lazily, leaning down and grinding out her cigarette on the tractor's metal mower attachment. "I just might have to get to know him better."

"I'd better get back to Starlight's grooming," Carole replied abruptly. "I barely have time to knock him off as it is." Keeping her head low to avoid Maureen's eyes, she grabbed a new bottle of antiseptic and hurried from the shed, not slowing her pace until she was back in the main building and approaching Starlight's stall.

Then she took a deep breath and slowed down. *What am I doing?* she wondered. Finding Maureen smoking in the equipment shed had gotten her so worked up that her hands were shaking. Or was it running into Ben that had done that?

She shook her head, suddenly annoyed with herself. Why was she wasting so much energy on this? Yes, the smoking thing was a real problem, and she would have to keep an eye on Maureen and decide what to do about that. But in the meantime, she had more interesting things to think about. Starting with the same topic that had been occupying her almost nonstop lately—namely, what on earth she was going to get Cam for Christmas.

FIVE

Stevie leaned against the hood of the two-door blue car she shared with her twin brother, Alex, who was tapping his fingers impatiently on the roof.

"Would you relax already?" Stevie complained, shooting him an annoyed glance. "The drum solo's getting old."

"What's taking Callie so long?" Alex demanded, checking his watch for about the twentieth time in the past thirty seconds. "I'm supposed to pick up Nicole in, like, ten minutes."

Stevie grimaced, wondering as she always did how her brother could possibly see anything in a total bimbo like Nicole Adams. It had been weird enough to think about Alex starting to date people other than Lisa. But Nicole? She had to be about as far from Lisa as it was possible to get without actually changing species.

But Stevie was trying not to think too much about it. She was sure that Alex would come to his senses soon. In the meantime, all she could do was watch and try not to be sick.

"Come on, Callie," Alex muttered, staring at his watch again. "Where is she, anyway? Fenton Hall's not that big."

"Chill! She'll be here, okay?" Stevie rolled her eyes. Alex had agreed to drop Stevie and Callie at Pine Hollow on his way home, since Scott had a student government officers' meeting that afternoon.

Turning to scan the crowds of students pouring out of the school building and scattering in all directions—heading for the parking lot, the waiting buses, and the pizza place across the street—Stevie didn't see any sign of Callie. She did notice George Wheeler emerging from the building, though she didn't think much about it. She'd been seeing quite a bit of George lately because of his crush on Callie, but normally the two of them barely qualified as acquaintances. If George hadn't been a regular at Pine Hollow, Stevie doubted she would even know his name.

To her surprise, George caught her eye and waved, turning and hurrying toward her. "Hi!" he called breathlessly as soon as he was within earshot. "How's it going, Stevie?"

"Fine, George," Stevie replied politely. "How are you?"

"Fine, fine!"

Great, Stevie thought. *Does this mean he has a crush on me now, too?*

"There she is!" Alex exclaimed, interrupting something George was starting to say about the weather. "Callie! Over here!"

Stevie glanced over and saw their friend hurrying down the school steps. "See? I told you she'd be here soon," she told her brother, poking him in the shoulder.

"Um, see you guys later," George muttered, spinning on his heel and walking quickly in the opposite direction.

Stevie blinked, wondering what had gotten into him. Then she shrugged. She didn't have time to stand around figuring out the likes of George Wheeler. Hurrying around to the passenger's side of the car, she opened the door and scooted into the backseat, leaving the door open for Callie.

Moments later the three of them were strapped in and Alex was peeling out of the school parking lot. "Hey, Speed Racer!" Stevie exclaimed, reaching forward to smack him on the back of the head. "Are you trying to get us all killed? This isn't the autobahn, you know."

Alex made a rude sound in response. "Okay, Grandma," he said sarcastically. He did slow down a little, though.

Satisfied, Stevie turned her attention to Callie. "So what's on your agenda for today?"

Callie sighed heavily and twisted around in her seat to face Stevie. "Oh, I'll probably spend most of it driving myself crazy trying to figure out what to do," she said. "I saw a great horse yesterday. I'm just not sure he's the *right* horse, if you know what I mean."

"Tell me," Stevie said eagerly.

"Well, his name's Scooby, and he's an Appaloosa." Callie went on to describe the gelding in detail, including her impressions while riding him the day before.

Stevie nodded thoughtfully as she listened. She knew that Callie took endurance competition seriously, and it was important for her to find the best horse she could. "All right," she said when her friend had finished. "That all sounds great. So what's the problem?"

"I just don't know if he's really as wonderful as I think he is."

Alex glanced at her. "Huh? You're going to have to translate that one."

"For once, my brother is right," Stevie said. "Explain."

Callie shrugged, her face twisted with uncertainty. "Yes, Scooby is a good horse, and I'm sure he

71

could do endurance. But I don't know if I'm making him out to be more talented than he is—in my own mind, I mean—just because I'm getting desperate to find a horse. There are one or two things that worry me a little. For example, Mr. Rayburn mentioned that Scooby is sometimes a little headstrong on the trails. And I'm not really used to Appaloosas, since just about every horse I've ridden in competition has been an Arabian or an Arabian cross. Anyway, I haven't really looked at that many horses yet, when you get right down to it. And I'm just thinking—I don't have any more appointments set up right now, so maybe I'm just trying to talk myself into this horse so that I don't have to start the whole process again."

"Ah." Stevie leaned back against her seat, thinking about that. She knew how Callie felt, sort of. Choosing a horse was a huge decision, and it didn't pay to make it lightly. There were a lot of things to consider, especially for someone like Callie, who needed a performance horse and not just a pleasure mount. Stevie herself had almost made a wrong choice or two before she'd found her perfect partner in Belle. "Okay, answer me this, then," she said to Callie seriously. "Did you start thinking he might be the one when you first saw him, or only after you got in the saddle?"

Callie pursed her lips and thought for a second.

"Well, I could tell his conformation was good from the ground," she said. "But that was true of a few of the others, too. I definitely started thinking he was a cut above when I was riding him."

"And did that opinion stay pretty much the same for the whole ride?" Stevie asked.

Callie shook her head. "It got stronger the more I rode him."

"Good. And what about the personality thing? Appaloosa or not, did he seem willing to work with you?"

This time Callie nodded immediately. "Definitely. He was right there with me pretty much from the time I mounted. A little testing, you know, but he settled right in."

Stevie shook her head and sighed. "Then I'm afraid I have some bad news for you."

Callie looked worried. "What?"

Stevie grinned. "I think you found yourself a horse!"

Alex snorted. "Tell us another one, O all-seeing Madame Stevie."

"No, actually I think she may be right," Callie said slowly. Stevie could tell that she was thinking hard. "Those were good questions. Better than the ones I've been asking myself." A smile spread across her face, lighting up her blue eyes. "I think you're right. I've found myself a horse!"

"*Whoo-hoo!*" Stevie crowed, raising her palm for a high five.

Callie obliged. "Thanks, Stevie," she said. "I guess I'd better get to work setting up a vet check. I'm going to call Mr. Rayburn as soon as I get to Pine Hollow and see when he can do it."

"Get ready to dial, then, 'cause we're here," Alex announced. "You guys will have to walk up from the road. I don't have time to stop."

"Okay, but at least slow down to thirty-five or so, okay?" Stevie said sarcastically, rolling her eyes at Callie. But she was grinning at the same time. She was really happy for Callie. Scooby sounded like a terrific horse for her, and Stevie knew that her friend would be a lot happier once she could start training for real instead of just noodling around with Barq.

The two girls hopped out of the car and hurried up Pine Hollow's long gravel drive together. Once inside the stable building, Callie turned off to use the pay phone near the office while Stevie headed across the entryway on her way to Belle's stall. She was feeling pretty good about herself—she'd helped her friend make an important decision, and it seemed to be the right one.

As she turned into the stable aisle, she saw Red about halfway down, talking to the new stable hand. Stevie had met Maureen the afternoon before, but she hadn't gotten much of an impression before one of the younger riders had dragged Maureen away with a question about fly spray. Now Stevie stopped short. Something about the way Maureen was standing—lounging against the nearest stall door, one hip stuck out and almost touching Red's leg—struck Stevie as somehow inappropriate.

She frowned, watching as Maureen leaned forward and put her hand on Red's upper arm, laughing at something he'd just said. *Isn't she standing a little close?* Stevie thought. *I mean, he's practically a married man. She doesn't have to hang all over him like that. What would Denise think if she—*

Just then Red looked up and spotted her. "Stevie!" he called, dislodging Maureen's hand as he waved. "There you are. Max wanted me to ask you if you could ride out and check the footing in that tricky spot on the trail—you know, right after it crosses the creek?"

"I'm on it," Stevie said immediately, pushing the disturbing little scene between Red and Maureen out of her mind. After all, Red loved Denise. Stevie knew that, and soon Maureen would realize it, too. Then she would figure out she'd better cool it with the touchy-feely stuff before someone got hurt.

". . . and I just don't understand how you can expect me to pick up and leave now!" Lisa cried, glaring at her mother from across the living room. "In case you've forgotten, it's my senior year!"

"I'm very well aware of that." Mrs. Atwood frowned and crossed her arms over her chest, sitting up primly on the sofa. "It would be difficult to forget, after the little matter of your college applications and all the mess that's come out of that whole situation."

Lisa felt like screaming. Instead, she clutched the wooden arms of her chair so tightly that her fingers started to go numb. When was her mother going to get over that? True, Lisa had decided to accept her admission to Northern Virginia University without telling her parents ahead of time. But what was the big deal, anyway? Lisa's mother knew she'd applied there. And NVU was a perfectly good school—Stevie's older brother, Chad, was a sophomore there, and Lisa knew plenty of other people who loved it. So what if Mrs. Atwood's snooty friends didn't think it was as good as some of the other universities on Lisa's list?

"We're not talking about my college plans right now, Mom," she said evenly. "We're talking about *your* plan to move us both to New Jersey."

"I'm aware of that, young lady." Mrs. Atwood frowned harder. "And you should be aware that in my opinion, it's all connected. I only wish I'd made this decision sooner. Then maybe you would have a different perspective on your future, and we wouldn't be in this mess right now."

Lisa clenched her hands into fists in her lap. She knew that her mother thought she'd decided to go to NVU only so that she could stay close to Alex. But that wasn't true. "Whatever," she said evenly. "When you get right down to it, it's my life we're talking about, and no matter what you think, I know I made the right decision."

Mrs. Atwood rolled her eyes dramatically. "I see," she said. "What does a mother know about life? How can I possibly argue with all the wisdom of your seventeen years?"

Just then the phone rang. "Saved by the bell," Lisa muttered.

"What was that, dear?" Mrs. Atwood asked sharply.

"I said I'll get it," Lisa replied, hurrying to grab the receiver. She took a deep breath as she picked it up, trying to calm herself down. "Hello, Atwood residence."

"Hi, Lisa." Scott Forester's voice came through the wire. "It's Scott. How are you?"

"Oh, hi. Um, hold on a second." Lisa put her hand over the mouthpiece and glanced at her mother. "It's for me."

"All right." Mrs. Atwood showed no signs of leaving the room. Instead, she picked up a real estate flyer from the coffee table and started flipping through it.

Gritting her teeth, Lisa removed her hand from the mouthpiece, wishing the phone were cordless. "Hi," she said. "What's up?"

"Not much," Scott said in his usual friendly, easy tone. "I was just calling to say hi, and to see if you made up your mind about that dinner yet. I was thinking we could take a ride out toward Berryville, maybe try that new Greek place everyone's talking about. What do you say?"

"Um . . ." Lisa glanced at her mother out of the corner of her eye. "I don't know."

"Come on," Scott wheedled teasingly. "I promise I won't make you try anything you can't pronounce."

"It's not that," Lisa said, more sharply than she'd intended. "I mean, I just don't think I can deal with this right now. I'm sorry."

"Oh." Scott sounded hurt, but he recovered quickly. "Okay, fair enough. Maybe I'll see you at the stable sometime this week. Catch you later."

"Bye." Lisa gently replaced the receiver, feeling guilty. After all, it wasn't Scott's fault that she was angry with her mother, and she had taken it out on him.

Oh well, she thought remorsefully. *Too late now. Anyway, I really can't deal with Scott today—at least that part was true. Not with everything else that's going on.*

Avoiding her mother's eye, she left the living room and hurried upstairs to her room, closing the door behind her and then flopping onto her bed. "What's wrong with me?" she murmured, burying her face in her pillow. "Why did my whole life decide to crash and burn all of a sudden?"

She didn't know the answer to that. It really did seem like a lot to handle all at once, especially with Christmas coming. . . .

Suddenly Lisa found herself blinking back tears. It just didn't seem fair. The holidays were supposed to be a happy time with family and friends, and here she was spending her days worrying about her future with Alex, snapping at people who were just trying to be nice to her, and fighting with her mother about moving.

Maybe I should just give in, agree to give up on it all and start over again in a new place like Mom wants me to, she thought, picking at the stitching on her pillow. *She thinks moving to New Jersey is going to solve all of her problems. And maybe she's right— maybe it really wouldn't be the worst thing in the world for me to get a fresh start, either.*

She shuddered and sat up straight on the bed, banishing the thought almost as soon as it had come. No way. She didn't want to start over. No matter how bleak things seemed at the moment, her best friends were still in Willow Creek. And that was enough.

Yes, she would find a way to stay in Willow Creek, in her *real* home, no matter what her mother said. She would just have to find a way to face her problems. She suspected that that would be a little easier after the holidays were over. This would have been her first Christmas with Alex, and now she didn't know if the two of them would ever be able to get back what they'd had together. It made the whole season seem bittersweet.

Hopping up, she walked over to the closet. There was a shopping bag on the top shelf; she pulled it down and dumped its contents onto the bed. Reaching out, she ran her fingers over the soft wool of the sweater she'd bought for Alex on her most recent trip to California. It was supposed to have been his Christmas present, but now she wondered if she would ever give it to him.

Her hand wandered to her throat, feeling for the necklace she already knew wasn't there. Soon after their breakup she'd stopped wearing the pendant Alex had bought her—it was across the room in her jewelry box, waiting for the day she might wear it again. She still remembered the day he'd given it to her. It had been her seventeenth birthday, and he'd looked so adorable as he'd bent down to fasten it around her neck . . .

No, she thought, staring at the sweater. *I'm not going to wallow in the past. I'm not going to give in to my doubts and regrets and all that stuff. That's no way to be happy. I've got to look forward instead—face the future. Be hopeful and optimistic that everything will work out if I just work at it hard enough.*

She grabbed the sweater and shoved it back into the bag. Then an idea struck her. The sweater had come from a national department store with a branch at the Willow Creek Mall. Dumping it out of the bag again, she shook it out until a thin white receipt fluttered out of its folds.

I'll start right away by returning this sweater, she thought resolutely, carefully folding the receipt and tucking it into her wallet so that it wouldn't get lost. *I can use the money to buy a wedding gift for Red and Denise instead. So while they're starting their new future, I can be starting mine, too.*

SIX

"*Twilight trail ride,*" Stevie muttered, tapping her pencil on her forehead. "*Trail ride at dusk? No, twilight trail ride.*" Jotting a quick note with her pencil, she turned back to the computer on her desk. She'd been barricaded in her bedroom ever since finishing dinner a half hour earlier, working feverishly on her article. It was due to the editor by Thursday, and Stevie didn't want to miss the deadline.

Pine Hollow's young riders look forward to the twilight trail ride all year long, she typed. *The Starlight Ride is a very special tradition, and everyone who has ever—*

The phone rang, interrupting her train of thought. Stevie glanced toward the door, expecting someone else to pick it up. It rang again. Remembering that she was the only one home—her parents had gone to a movie, and her brothers had disappeared somewhere or other—she jumped up and raced to grab the extension on her bedside table.

"Hello?" she said briskly.

"Stevie? Is that you? It's Carole."

Stevie wrinkled her nose and pressed the phone closer to her ear. "Carole? I can hardly hear you," she said. "What's all that noise in the background?"

"I'm at a pay phone at the mall," Carole explained, raising her voice slightly. "Dad needed to pick up some shoes, so I tagged along to try to find a Christmas present for Cam. But I'm not having much luck so far."

Stevie chewed her lip impatiently, at least half her mind still on her article. She wanted to be supportive, but why was Carole calling her? Lisa was much more of an expert shopper than she was.

"Anyway, I thought about calling Lisa for advice," Carole said, as if reading her mind. "But I thought shopping for, you know, a *guy* might—well, you know."

Stevie nodded, suddenly understanding. Lisa was probably a little sensitive about that topic at the moment, and no wonder. "Um, you still have, like, two weeks until you and Cam are exchanging gifts, right? So there's no huge hurry. Maybe you should look around a little more there, kind of get some ideas," she suggested. "Then we can discuss it in a couple of days." *After my article is finished,* she added silently.

"Well . . . okay," Carole said, though she sounded reluctant. "I guess that makes sense. Thanks, Stevie."

"Anytime. See you," Stevie said, relieved. She hung up the phone and returned to her desk. Flopping into her chair, she stared blankly at the computer screen, trying to gather her thoughts. After a moment she started to type again.

. . . ridden along on this magical night will remember it always.

Stevie sat back and read over what she'd written so far. "No," she muttered. "That doesn't really work." Deleting the last sentence, she tried again.

The Starlight Ride is such a special tradition that it lives in the memories of all who have experienced it. Maximilian Regnery III, the owner of Pine Hollow Stables, held the first Starlight Ride eleven years ago. It was—

The phone rang again. "Shoot," Stevie muttered, quickly hitting Save and heading across the room again. "Hello!" she said. "Lake house."

"Hey, it's me," Phil's familiar voice responded. "What's up?"

"I'm kind of in the middle of my article right now," Stevie told him. "So I really should—"

"Okay, okay," Phil interrupted with a chuckle. "I

get the hint. I'll make this quick. I was just calling to tell you that A.J. decided to try to track down that woman."

Stevie gasped, momentarily forgetting her impatience. "Really? That's great!"

"I know. He's nervous, obviously, but I think he's kind of excited, too."

A million and one questions tumbled through Stevie's brain. How was A.J. going to find that woman? What was he going to say if he did? What would happen if she really was his birth mother?

But Stevie knew her curiosity would have to wait a little longer. Somehow, she didn't think that someone else's family crisis was going to cut it as an excuse to the editor if Stevie missed her deadline. "Listen, thanks for the update," she told Phil reluctantly. "I'm dying to hear all about it, you know I am. But my article . . . I'd really better go. We'll talk about this soon, though, okay?"

"Definitely. Good luck with your article."

"Thanks." Stevie hung up and then stood there for a couple of seconds, trying to imagine how A.J. must be feeling. It had to be a tough time for him, though Stevie was glad he'd decided to face his past instead of avoiding it.

Returning to her desk, she sat down and flexed her fingers. Then she resumed typing.

. . . such a success that it has continued ever since.

She paused and pawed through the messy stack of notes on the desk beside the computer. She'd jotted down ideas for the article whenever they came to her, which meant that her desk was currently littered with scrap paper, napkins, and even the label from a package of fly tape. "Where is that quote from Max?" she muttered.

Before she located what she was looking for, a familiar ring interrupted. "What is this, the central switchboard of Willow Creek?" she cried. Leaping to her feet, she raced over to the phone again. "Hello?"

"Hey, it's Scott. Stevie?"

"Yeah, it's me." Stevie glanced at her watch. With all these interruptions, she was never going to finish. "What's going on?"

"Uh, not much, I guess." Scott sounded uncharacteristically subdued. "I was just, well . . ." His voice trailed off.

"Spit it out," Stevie demanded, too impatient for tact. "What's up?"

Scott sighed heavily into the phone. "I was hoping for some advice," he said. "I know this is a little awkward, since you're Alex's sister and all, but I wasn't sure who else to ask."

"Ask what?"

"Do you think I have a shot with Lisa?" Scott asked. "I mean, I just called to see if she wanted to grab some chow this weekend or something, and she was kind of, I don't know. . . ."

Stevie groaned under her breath. She *really* didn't have time for this. Since when had she become Dear Abby, anyway? "Listen," she said briskly. "I know Lisa pretty well, and she's kind of sensitive. You know, like to how people say things, that sort of stuff. So if you actually said, 'Hey, let's grab some chow,' it's no wonder she's not chomping at the bit to go out with you."

"I wasn't quite that bad." Scott sounded a bit wounded. "Actually, I invited her out to that new place in Berryville."

Stevie rolled her eyes. Guys could be so clueless sometimes. "That's nice," she said carefully. "But it's something any guy might suggest. Why don't you come up with something a little more romantic?" She grimaced, not quite sure why she was advising Scott on this. *It's not as if he really has a chance in the long run,* she thought. *Lisa and Alex will probably get back together in a couple of weeks, and that will be that. Of course, it might not go quite so smoothly if my big mouth means Scott is in the picture by then, making things more complicated.*

Trying not to think about that too much, she said good-bye and hung up. She'd hardly reached her desk when the phone rang again. Spinning on her heel, she raced over and grabbed it.

"Yes?" she snapped into the mouthpiece. "Lake residence."

"What's the matter?" Lisa's voice asked. "You sound upset."

"No, it's nothing." Stevie slumped against the edge of the bed. "I'm just working on my article. Uh, I guess I was kind of in the zone when you called, that's all."

"Oh." Lisa sounded a little sad. "Sorry to interrupt. I was just calling to say hi. I'll let you go if you need to get back to work."

Stevie hesitated, torn. It didn't take a genius of a best friend to guess that Lisa was feeling sad, which meant that she was probably worrying about her mother's plan to move. Stevie wanted to help, but she also wanted to finish her article sometime before graduation. Glancing from the phone to her desk and back again, she suddenly thought of a way to distract Lisa from her gloom. "Hey, guess who just called a few minutes ago?" she said brightly.

"Who?"

"Your not-so-secret admirer, Scott," Stevie said. She hoped she wasn't making a complicated situation even stickier by mentioning Scott's call, but desperate times called for desperate measures. She could deal with the Alex-Lisa-Scott triangle later, after her article was finished. For the moment, all she wanted was to give Lisa something to think about—

something that might distract her from her problems with her mother. "He was looking for advice on how to win your heart."

"Really?" Lisa sounded hesitant.

"Uh-huh." Stevie checked her watch and grimaced. "But listen, can we talk about it some more tomorrow? I really do need to get back to work. Sorry."

"No, I'm sorry," Lisa said quickly. "Go ahead, I understand. I'll talk to you later."

"Okay. Bye." As soon as she sat down at her desk, Stevie spotted the piece of paper she'd been looking for before Scott's call. "Aha," she muttered triumphantly. Propping it up against her stapler, she quickly resumed her typing.

"Pine Hollow has a lot of traditions, but the Starlight Ride is truly special," Mr. Regnery told this reporter recently, echoing the feelings of many young riders over the years. The—

RRRING! RRRRRING!

"I don't believe this!" Pushing her chair back so abruptly that it nearly toppled over, Stevie stomped over to her bedside table and grabbed the phone. "Hello? This better be important!" she yelped.

"Stevie? Is that you?"

"Callie?" Stevie felt guilty. After all, it wasn't her friends' fault she was on a deadline. "Um, hi. Sorry about that. The phone, uh, caught me by surprise."

"That's okay," Callie said, sounding more animated than usual. "Listen, I just got off the phone with Mr. Rayburn—you know, Scooby's owner? And it's all worked out. I'm meeting Judy Barker tomorrow after school, and if Scooby vets out okay, he could be mine by Friday afternoon!"

"Really?" All thoughts of her article flew out of Stevie's mind at the news. "That's fantastic! I'm sure he'll pass the vet check with flying colors."

"I sure hope so," Callie said with an anxious sigh. "I'll be sitting on pins and needles until then. Oops! There's call waiting. It may be Judy confirming the time—I'd better go."

This time as Stevie hung up, she was left feeling unsatisfied by the phone call. Picking up the receiver again, she quickly dialed Lisa's number. *I've just got to tell someone about Callie's great news*, she thought with a guilty glance at the computer. *It will only take a sec. . . .*

She heard her friend's familiar voice on the other end of the line. "Hey, Lisa, it's me again," she said quickly. "Guess what?"

The following afternoon after last period, Callie was jogging down the crowded school hallway toward her locker when she almost collided with Stevie, who was emerging from a nearby classroom. "Hi!" Stevie greeted her, looking distracted. "Where are you off to in such a hurry this aftern—Oh! Today's Scooby's vet check, isn't it?"

"Uh-huh." Forcing her mind off the coming hours long enough to recall what was going on in Stevie's life, Callie glanced at the sheaf of papers in her friend's hand. "Are you heading upstairs to turn in your article?"

Stevie lifted the papers and shrugged. "Not exactly. I didn't accomplish as much as I wanted to last night. I'll probably have to pull an all-nighter tonight. But it'll be worth it—it's going to knock Theresa's socks off when it's finished. Not to mention the rest of the school. Max will probably have to buy a dozen new horses to keep up with all the people who are going to want to come along on this year's Starlight Ride after they read about it."

Callie grinned, delighted as she always was at Stevie's ebullient self-confidence. She had often thought that if there were a way to bottle her friend's aplomb, high school would be a whole lot easier for a lot of people. "Cool," she said. "I can't wait to read it."

"But what about you?" Stevie grabbed Callie's arm and grinned. "You must be practically fainting with excitement. Are you nervous?"

"Definitely. But I'm psyched, too." Callie swallowed hard to calm the butterflies rampaging in her stomach. Her anxiety had been fighting it out with

91

her euphoria since the day before. Now that she'd decided that Scooby was the right horse for her, all doubts about her choice were gone. The only thing that could derail her now was if something went wrong that afternoon. "If Judy doesn't find anything unexpected, like heart or lung problems or an artificial leg or something, Scooby will be mine!"

"Don't worry," Stevie said reassuringly. "I'm sure he's as healthy as a—well, you know." She winked and grinned.

"Thanks." Callie took a deep, calming breath. "I hope you're right. Judy's not an endurance specialist, but I'm pretty sure she can tell me whether Scooby's up to the job."

"Absolutely," Stevie declared. "Judy's the best equine vet around. She'll go over Scooby with a fine-tooth comb until you're satisfied that he's just as perfect as you think he is."

"I hope you're right," Callie said again. "I'd better get going. I'm supposed to meet her over there in twenty minutes."

"Good luck. Let me know what happens."

Callie gave a little wave and spun on her heel to head for the nearest exit. As she turned, she caught a flash of movement off to the left, among all the activity of the hall. Glancing that way, she saw George walking quickly in the opposite direction.

She frowned, oddly disturbed. Had he been staring at her while she was talking to Stevie?

Get real, Paranoid Girl, she told herself sharply. *George goes to school here, too, remember? He has every right to walk down the hall.*

She shrugged, guessing that her anxiety over the vet check was making her a little jumpy. And after all, George was finally doing what she wanted—staying away from her, both at school and at the stable.

"Speaking of stables . . . ," she muttered, remembering what she was supposed to be doing. Scooby was waiting. She headed for the door at a brisk walk, all thoughts of George Wheeler flying out of her mind.

SEVEN

"Do you have an extra pen?" Carole whispered to Cam, shooting a quick glance at the main desk at the front of Willow Creek Public Library's reading room. "Mine just ran out of ink."

"Sure." Cam dug a ballpoint out of his backpack, then held it up just out of her reach with a teasing gleam in his dark eyes. "But it doesn't come for free."

Carole giggled, then cast another worried glance toward the front desk. The librarian had his back to her as he helped another student find something on the computer. "Okay, will you give it to me if I do this?" she said, leaning over to plant a kiss on his waiting lips.

"Mmm," Cam murmured through the kiss. "That's more like it."

Carole finally broke away a minute or two later when she opened her eyes and noticed a group of students at the next table giving them dirty looks.

Blushing, she sat back in her chair and smoothed her hair, which had become slightly rumpled under Cam's caress. "Um, anyway, thanks," she said, grabbing the pen out of his hand and willing her heartbeat to slow down to its normal pace. Searching her mind for an innocuous topic, she cleared her throat. "So I forgot to ask. Did you come up with any brilliant ideas yet about how to convince Dad to let us go on the Starlight Ride together?"

"I'm doing my best," Cam replied. "Don't worry, I'll find a way. I'm already looking forward to riding along with you by torchlight. It's going to be great."

"Definitely," Carole whispered.

She was sure that Cam would be as good as his word. In the days since they'd become a couple, he'd shown a real talent for finding creative ways to convince her father to let them spend time together in spite of her grounding. That day, for instance, he had helped Carole convince her father that they should study together. Carole had been a little surprised when he'd agreed readily, with no arguments or *only ifs*.

I guess Dad thinks Cam is a good influence on me, she thought, sneaking a peek at Cam as he bent over his schoolbooks. *And you know what? I think he's right. I know I've been a lot happier since he moved back to Virginia. Being with him makes my whole life seem better.*

Cam glanced up and caught her staring. She blushed, but he just smiled and reached for her hand. "Hey, I just realized I need to find a book," he whispered. "Want to come help me look?"

"Sure." Carole got up and followed him toward the stacks. Cam ducked into the first aisle, pulling her along to the end of the row.

"Aha," Cam said in a low, husky voice. "I think I just spotted what I need—right here." He grabbed her around the waist and pulled her close, bending down to seek out her lips with his own.

Carole closed her eyes and felt herself getting swept away. Would she ever get tired of kissing Cam? She seriously doubted it.

She came back to earth when she heard a throat being cleared loudly nearby. Her eyes flew open and she jumped away from Cam. The assistant librarian was standing at the end of the row, glaring at them sternly. "Do you mind?" she said crisply. "This is a library, not a cheap motel room."

"S-sorry," Carole stammered, her face flaming. "Uh, we—"

"We're sorry, ma'am," Cam said. "We'll behave from now on, we promise."

"See that you do." The woman frowned. "Otherwise you'll have to leave the library."

Carole wasn't sure she'd ever been more humiliated. She was ready to make the librarian's wish come true and run out of the building then and there, never to return. But Cam grinned as soon as the woman was out of sight. "Oops," he said. "Guess we got busted."

"Maybe we should go back to the table and get back to studying," Carole said nervously. She couldn't even begin to imagine what her father would say if they got caught kissing again and the librarian decided to call their parents.

"I've got a better idea." Cam took her hand again. Peeking past the end of the row to make sure the coast was clear, he led Carole in the opposite direction, deeper into the stacks. Soon they were in the very last row near the emergency exit. Nobody else was in sight.

Cam ran his hand up her arm, cupped her neck, and pulled her gently toward him. "There," he whispered, holding her gaze as he dipped his face toward hers. "Now we can really get some studying done."

Stevie leaned her chin on her hand, staring at the computer screen in front of her. *I wonder if Phil's as bummed as I am that I had to cancel our date today*, she thought grumpily. *I can't believe my article still isn't finished.*

She sighed, knowing it was her own fault. She'd gotten so caught up in all those phone calls the night before that she'd hardly written anything.

Now it was Wednesday afternoon and she had no choice. She had to finish that night if she wanted the article to be published.

And I do, she reminded herself, tapping the arrow key to scroll down through what she had written. *It's turning out really well so far, and I'm sure Theresa will love it. I just wish there was an extra day in the week so that I could finish writing it and see Phil.*

It was bad enough to have to give up a chance to get together with Phil—since they went to different schools, they never seemed to have enough time together—but now she would also have to wait to find out what was happening with A.J. Knowing that he was trying to track down the woman who might be his biological mother made her more curious than ever.

"Oh well," she muttered, trying to forget about that for the moment and focus on her article. "Back to the grindstone." She sat up straight, thought for a moment, and then started typing.

Max and his crew lay out the path through the woods in advance, marking the way with flickering torches that add to the magical ambiance. As they ride, participants sometimes sing holiday songs, while at other times they simply ride in silence, enjoying the extraordinary feeling of being with special friends in the hushed beauty of the winter woods.

Sitting back with a smile, Stevie read over the last

few lines again. Just writing them had reminded her of all the times she'd gone on the Starlight Ride and how much fun she and her friends had always had.

Her mind wandered to Phil again. She couldn't wait to see his face when he opened the incredible gift she was getting him. Alex and Michael had already agreed to her money-for-presents plan, and Stevie figured she'd have no trouble convincing Chad when he arrived home for the holidays the following Monday night. She intended to hit The Saddlery that weekend and buy the chaps.

Nothing like a little last-minute Christmas shopping, she thought ruefully, realizing that Christmas Eve was only six days away. *Still, I've been so busy lately that I've hardly been able to find the time to eat and sleep, let alone stroll the mall.*

Thinking about everything she'd accomplished over the past couple of weeks—working on her article, helping Max with Starlight Ride preparations, dealing with various friends' problems, and of course keeping up with her usual load of chores and homework—made her look forward to Christmas Eve more than ever. The Starlight Ride would be the perfect reward to herself for surviving her own busy life.

It's going to be so great, she thought with a happy sigh, scanning the last part of her article again. *Whatever made me think the Starlight Ride was just*

*kids' stuff? Life couldn't possibly get better than that—
me and Phil, riding along through the woods in the
crisp Christmas Eve twilight. Oh, and helping Max
and the others deal with a whole bunch of giggly pre-
teen riders, of course.* She grinned at the thought.
Who would have thought that hanging out with
May Grover, Sarah Anne Porter, and the rest of the
intermediate riding brats would ever sound like a romantic evening?

Picturing herself and Phil riding along through
the December evening, she wondered if she should
give her boyfriend his gift before the ride. It was sure
to be chilly out there in the woods after dark, and
those chaps could come in handy.

But she shook her head almost immediately. *Better stick to the original plan,* she decided. *Our gift exchange will be a lot more intimate after the ride, when
we won't be constantly interrupted by intermediate
riders looking for someone to help tighten their girth or
find them a spare pair of stirrup leathers.*

She could picture it already. She and Phil would
find a cozy spot in Belle's stall or maybe up in the
hayloft. He would insist that she open her gift first,
and she would ooh and aah appropriately over whatever he got her.

Then it will be his turn, she thought gleefully.
*He'll rip the paper off in one motion like he always does
and immediately recognize the box from The Saddlery.*

So he'll go to open it, assuming it's a new saddle pad or something like that. It'll probably take him a second or two to realize what's really inside—that's when he'll gasp in stunned, rapturous disbelief and tell me what a superfabulous, one-of-a-kind, downright amazing girlfriend I am. . . .

As she imagined Phil's response, she shifted her weight and accidentally hit the keyboard on the desk. It blooped in protest, and she blinked, suddenly remembering that she had work to do before she could move on to making Phil's dreams come true. Shaking her head to clear the image of her boyfriend's ecstatic face out of her mind, she sighed and returned her attention to the computer screen.

EIGHT 8

"Hello?" Lisa peered over the half door into Belle's stall. "Stevie? You in there?"

But the only one in the roomy stall was Stevie's friendly mare, who blinked at Lisa quizzically and continued chewing a mouthful of hay. Lisa leaned on the door and sighed, watching the horse for a moment. She had come straight over to Pine Hollow after school, hoping to find some company to take her mind off her problems. But there was no sign of Stevie, Carole, or Callie anywhere.

Oh well, she thought, disappointed. *I guess I should get used to being lonely. If Mom has her way, this is going to be a familiar feeling soon.*

She walked slowly down the aisle, pausing to pat a few favorite horses on her way. When she emerged into the entryway, she was just in time to see Callie disappearing into the locker room. Scott was stand-

102

ing in the doorway, his car keys in his hand. He smiled slightly when he saw her.

Lisa gulped. She still felt bad about snapping at him on the phone two days earlier. She hadn't seen or spoken to him since then, and she knew it was time to make things right. She stepped toward him. "Scott, I'm glad you're—" she began.

"Wait." Scott held up a hand, his voice commanding. "Me first."

"But I just want to explain about the other day," Lisa protested quickly. "When you asked me about dinner—"

"Never mind that." Scott shook his head. "I don't want to take you to dinner over in Berryville anymore."

Lisa blinked. "Huh? Y-you don't?" she stammered uncertainly. "But I was just going to tell you—I mean I . . ." She wasn't sure what to say.

Scott took a step toward her. "No, I changed my mind about that," he said. "Instead of taking you to dinner in Berryville, I would rather take you to see *The Nutcracker*. In D.C. This Saturday night." He reached into his pocket and produced two colorful strips of cardboard. Tickets. "And if that goes well, perhaps you'll allow me to be your date for the Starlight Ride next week. What do you say?"

Lisa opened and closed her mouth several times,

her head spinning. *The Nutcracker?* The Starlight Ride? "Um . . . That's so generous," she murmured, playing for time so that she could figure out what to say.

What did she want to say? She had no idea. With the way she was feeling lately, wondering if she was going to be forced in a few short weeks to leave the life and home she'd always known, she was tempted just to forget about dating altogether. Why bother? Every Saturday night she spent with a guy—even a cute, charming, strangely compelling one like Scott Forester—was another night she wouldn't get to hang out with her friends. And being with them just seemed like the most important thing in the world to her right then.

She was trying to figure out how to explain all that without hurting Scott's feelings when the door flew open and Stevie rushed in, breathless and pink-cheeked. "Yo!" she cried exuberantly. "Is this a fantastic day or what?"

Scott smiled at her, seemingly unperturbed by the interruption. "Hey, Lake," he said. "What's so great about it?"

Stevie stuck out her tongue at him. "As if you didn't know." She spun to face Lisa. "I just got out of a *Sentinel* meeting," she said. "And Theresa and the others loved my article! It's going to run in tomorrow's issue!"

"That's great!" Lisa said, sincerely pleased for her friend. Stevie's new interest in being a reporter had come on suddenly, but she really seemed to be serious about it. "Congratulations. I can't wait to read it."

"Thanks." Stevie smiled happily, shifting her backpack from one shoulder to the other. "I'm pretty psyched about it myself. Phil and I are going out Saturday night to celebrate—and it's about time, too. I feel like we haven't had a real date in ages." She rolled her eyes dramatically.

"Oh." Lisa's heart sank. So much for hanging out with her two best friends on Saturday night. Still, maybe she could make do with one. "So does that mean you're not planning on double-dating with Carole and Cam?" she asked, trying to sound casual.

Stevie shrugged. "I think this weekend is her big shopping extravaganza with the colonel," she said, referring to Carole's father, who had recently retired from the Marine Corps.

"Oh, right," Lisa muttered. "I forgot about that." A few days earlier at school, Carole had mentioned that she and her father were planning to drive to an outlet mall in North Carolina that Saturday, where they would do some last-minute holiday shopping and then have dinner before driving home.

She bit back a sigh. *Oh well,* she thought. *I guess I can't expect my friends to put their lives on hold just because my whole life might be changing soon.* She knew she was being a little melodramatic. But she couldn't help feeling sorry for herself. Both her best friends were at the beginning of exciting new parts of their lives—Stevie with the school newspaper and Carole with her new romance. It didn't seem fair that Lisa might have to miss seeing how it all turned out.

At that moment Red O'Malley strode out of the office hallway. "Stevie!" he exclaimed. "You're here."

"In the flesh," Stevie replied. "What do you need me to do?"

"Max called the farrier in to check everyone's shoes before the Starlight Ride," Red said. "As usual, Eve is being spooky about it. We need someone to hold her. Then Max wants you to make a sign and a wall envelope for the student locker room where riders can turn in their permission slips."

Stevie shot Lisa and Scott an apologetic grin. "Duty calls," she said lightly. Pausing just long enough to fling her backpack in the general direction of the locker room, she hurried after Red, leaving Lisa alone with Scott once again.

"So, where were we?" Scott said with a slight smile. "Oh, right. You were just about to tell me how you'd love to go to the ballet with me on Saturday."

Lisa smiled back weakly. It wasn't as if she had a

whole lot of other options. And staying home to argue with her mother some more wasn't really her idea of a fun Saturday night. Besides, she had always loved *The Nutcracker,* and this would be her only chance to see it this year. "You're right," she said. "I was just going to say that."

"Great!" Scott's eyes lit up. "Does that mean you're saying yes to the Starlight Ride, too?"

"I'll have to think about that," Lisa replied hastily. She wasn't sure how to express it to Scott, but the idea of a date for the Starlight Ride seemed more than a little weird. It had always been an event geared toward the younger riders at the stable—she couldn't remember anyone over the age of fifteen ever going unless they were acting as a chaperone for the little kids. Still, she supposed Scott couldn't really be expected to know that. This would be his first Christmas in Willow Creek, and the way Stevie and Carole kept talking about bringing their boyfriends along on the Starlight Ride this year, it shouldn't come as a surprise that Scott had the impression it was some kind of hot romantic thing. "Maybe we can talk about it after the ballet," she added tactfully.

"Fair enough." Scott gave a little bow and smiled. "I'll pick you up at six-fifteen, okay?"

"Sounds great," Lisa replied.

Scott took another step toward her. He was

standing so close that Lisa could smell his after-shave—spicy and sharp, like the cloves her mother sometimes used for baking. "Until Saturday, then," he said softly, leaning toward her.

His polite kiss grazed her cheek. But then, somehow, he didn't quite pull away. And Lisa found her head turning slightly until her lips met his.

What am I doing? she thought desperately as Scott's arms encircled her and pulled her against him. She wondered if he could hear her heart galloping like a runaway horse inside her chest. *What are* we *doing?*

Then she stopped thinking about it and just went with the feeling.

"Whoo-hoo!" a loud voice interrupted them a minute or two later. "Get a room, you two!"

Lisa broke away with a gasp, then turned and saw Maureen Chance grinning at them. The new stable hand was leaning against the door to the indoor ring, one booted foot crossed over the other.

Scott cleared his throat. "Hey, Maureen," he said, sounding surprisingly normal. "We didn't see you come in."

"Obviously," Maureen drawled. "Looked like you two were pretty busy."

"We were just, er, talking," Scott said sheepishly, though he was smiling as he said it.

Lisa didn't know how he could stay so calm. She

could feel her own face burning. Had she lost her mind? What was she doing standing around in the middle of a public stable making out like that? What if it had been Max who had happened along and caught them? What if it had been Alex?

Maureen stood up straight and came toward them. "I can see I'm going to have to keep an eye on you, Mr. Forester," she said teasingly. "I could tell from the first time I laid eyes on you that you were trouble. And here you are, already getting poor little—" She paused, obviously searching her mind. "Lisa, is it?—in trouble. Of course, I can't say I blame her." She smirked and sidled a little closer to Scott. "Who could resist such a big, strapping boy?"

Scott smiled. "Aw, shucks. You're going to make me blush, Miz Chance."

Lisa frowned, irritated by the way Maureen was blatantly flirting with Scott. *What's her problem? For all she knows, Scott and I could be some really serious couple. And she's acting like it's open season.*

Deciding to make her exit before she managed to embarrass herself further by snapping at Maureen, she cleared her throat. "Excuse me," she muttered. "I've got to get going."

Scott winked and smiled at Lisa as she turned to leave, but Maureen hardly bothered to glance her way. Lisa clenched her teeth and hurried toward the stable aisle, wondering why she was getting so upset.

It's not as if Scott and I really are a couple, she reminded herself. *We're just a couple of friends who are going out on a couple of dates. That's all.*

She couldn't resist glancing over her shoulder just before she turned the corner into the aisle. Back in the entryway, Maureen had her hand on Scott's arm. He was still giving her his most charming smile, as if there were nothing the slightest bit strange about the fact that a twenty-five-year-old woman was flirting with a high school senior. Lisa shook her head, wondering if she'd made a big mistake by agreeing to go out with him again.

Then she turned away and continued into the aisle, deciding it was too late to second-guess herself now. She would go to *The Nutcracker* with Scott on Saturday night and take it from there. Maybe that was all it would take for the two of them to figure out that they were better off as friends.

And if not, Lisa thought, a blush creeping back up her cheeks as she remembered that kiss, *well, we'll just have to figure out how to deal with it then.*

Carole stared at the glossy photograph of a hand-knit Irish fisherman's sweater, trying to picture how it would look on Cam. Finally she shook her head, deciding it really wasn't his style. Flipping quickly through the rest of the catalog, she tossed it on the growing pile of rejects beside her on the living room floor.

"Next," she muttered, grabbing another catalog from the coffee table. She had been looking for gift ideas since arriving home from school. She knew it was probably too late to order Cam's gift through the mail—unless she wanted to spend as much on priority shipping as she did on the gift itself—but she figured checking out what the catalogs had to offer would give her some inspiration before she hit the outlet stores with her father that weekend.

"Anybody home?" her father's voice sang out from the front hall.

"In here, Dad," Carole called back, looking up as he walked into the room, still wearing a wool coat over his dark business suit. In addition to giving motivational speeches at businesses all over the country, Colonel Hanson was on the board of several charities and other organizations. "How was your meeting?"

"Just fine." Shrugging off his coat, Colonel Hanson leaned over to plant a kiss on her forehead. He cast a curious look at the stacks of catalogs. "What are you up to? Making your list for Santa?"

"I'm trying to figure out what to get Cam for Christmas." Carole sighed heavily. "But all the really nice stuff is so expensive. Um, is there any way I could get a little advance on my allowance if I need it?"

Her father slung his coat over a chair, then sat on the couch. "I thought you still had some money saved for presents."

"I do." Carole shrugged, flipping quickly through another catalog and thinking of those chaps Stevie was buying for Phil. "But I'm afraid it won't be enough. I want to get Cam something really special."

"Special, huh?" Her father smiled slightly. "Is that a synonym for *expensive*?"

Carole hardly heard him. She had just realized what she should have seen sooner—she needed a man's opinion on what to buy for a man. "Hey, Dad," she said eagerly, dropping the catalog she was holding and scooting a little closer to the couch. "What was the best, most special gift you ever got? Your very favorite?"

"My favorite gift?" Colonel Hanson scratched his chin contemplatively. "Well, I loved the briefcase you got me last year. And of course your mother gave me some wonderful gifts when she was alive— she always managed to surprise me. But as for my very favorite? I'd have to say it was the macaroni horse you made for me in second grade."

"Really?" Carole knew exactly which macaroni

horse he meant. It had suffered some wear and tear through the years—for instance, there was the time Carole's cat had knocked it under the bed, breaking off one of its ears—but it still sat in a place of honor on top of his bureau. Carole had never really thought about it, since it had been there for ages, but now she realized it wasn't exactly the kind of decoration most adults would choose for their bedroom. Not without reason, anyway. It made her feel good to realize that her father kept it there because she had made it for him.

"What about you?" her father asked. "Which gifts have meant the most to you?"

"Oh, I don't know." Carole shrugged thoughtfully, still thinking about that macaroni horse. "I pretty much like everything. Like the new turnout rug you got me for my birthday. Or the nice leather halter Stevie gave me last Christmas." Then she remembered another gift from the previous Christmas. "Oh! But I really liked that ceramic tree ornament Denise made for me. Remember? The one shaped like Starlight. She painted the right markings on it and everything." Her gaze wandered to the corner where she and her father put up a small Christmas tree every year. Suddenly she couldn't wait to get that year's tree. "That ornament was probably my favorite gift last year."

"Really?" Her father looked interested. "But a handmade ornament can't possibly have cost as much as a turnout rug or a leather halter."

Carole rolled her eyes and laughed. "Real subtle, Dad," she said. "I get it. It was special because Denise made it just for me."

She paused and thought about that for a moment. Now that she put her mind to it, she started to remember a lot of extra-special gifts she'd received over the years. A hand-sewn teddy bear from her mother. A framed photograph of Starlight that Lisa had taken herself. A well-worn horse-shaped amulet from her great-grandmother. Even an almost inedible batch of pony-shaped cookies that Stevie had made from scratch.

"Okay, all joking aside," Carole said, remembering how she'd saved those cookies until they'd crumbled and started to smell. "The very best gifts I've ever gotten have really never been the most expensive ones, you know?"

Her father cocked an eyebrow at her, a slight smile playing around the edges of his mouth. "Oh?"

Realizing what he was thinking, Carole giggled. "Okay, okay," she corrected herself hastily. "Except for Starlight." Her father had bought Starlight for her one Christmas several years earlier, and Carole had to admit that the spirited gelding had been the best gift she could possibly imagine.

Colonel Hanson grinned. "I know what you mean, though, sweetie," he said. "It's kind of a cliché to say it's the thought that counts, but that doesn't mean it isn't true. That's just something to think about while you're searching for the perfect gift for Cam."

"Thanks, Dad," Carole said as her father stood and picked up his coat again, heading toward the front hall closet.

Carole sat back against the couch, thinking about what really made a gift special. *It's that heartfelt personal touch,* she thought. *That's what I want Cam to see—that whatever I give him is for him alone, from me alone. It has to let him know how happy I am that we've found each other again.*

That seemed like a pretty tall order. Glancing at the stacks of catalogs, Carole realized she was looking in the wrong place.

Most of the really great gifts in my life have been handmade, she reminded herself, standing up and wandering toward the stairs. *So maybe I could try making Cam an ornament or something, like the one from Denise. Or baking him his favorite kind of cake. Or maybe writing him a poem.*

She stopped short. A poem! That was it! What better way to let Cam know how she felt about him than to put it into actual words?

"It's perfect," Carole murmured, a smile spreading across her face as she pictured his reaction. Cam was such a romantic—a love poem would be the best gift in the world for him!

Hurrying up to her room, she sat down at her desk and pulled out a pen and a writing tablet. Chewing the end of the pen for a moment, she thought about what she wanted to express. Then she bent over and started to write.

I'm really glad you moved back, Cam
I really, truly am

She read over what she'd written. Then she snorted and crumpled the paper. Turning to a fresh page, she stared thoughtfully into space before trying again.

Cam, I'm so glad we are together
We're like birds of a feather
My love is bright in any weather

"Aaargh!" Carole cried, slashing through the sappy words with an angry stroke of her pen. "How do those professional poets *do* this, anyway?"

She tossed the tablet and pen aside, discouraged. What in the world had made her think her poetry plan was going to work? Now that she thought about it, she'd never received anything higher than a

B-minus on any poem she'd ever written for English class.

Okay, so maybe I'm not meant to be the next Shakespeare, she thought, leaning back in her desk chair with a sigh. *But I still think it's a good idea to give Cam something personal, something he'll really appreciate because it could come only from me.* She sighed again. *I just wish I knew what that was.*

NINE

"Don't worry, Callie, I do have my license," Red commented, glancing over from the driver's seat of his truck as he stopped at a red light. "And I'm doing my very best not to kill us."

Callie blinked. She had no idea what he was talking about. Then she glanced down and saw that her knuckles were white from clutching her armrest so hard. "Oh. Sorry," she said sheepishly, loosening her grip. "I guess I'm just nervous."

"I know. And I'm just teasing," Red said with a smile as the light changed and he put the truck into gear. "Buying a horse is exciting, but it's also nerve-wracking, especially when you don't even have the critter home yet."

Callie nodded her agreement. The two of them were heading for Mr. Rayburn's farm with Pine Hollow's smallest horse trailer hooked behind the truck. The day had finally arrived. Scooby had come through his vet check with flying colors, and now

Callie was riding over to pick him up and bring him back to Pine Hollow, his new home. She planned to spend the day getting better acquainted and making her new horse feel at home. If all went well, they could start some preliminary training the next day.

Fearing that she might burst with excitement if she thought about that any longer, she glanced over at Red and changed the subject. "You know, I'm not the only one taking on new responsibilities these days," she said. "What about you? Are you psyched for the big wedding? It's only, like, ten days away, right?"

"Eleven." Red shifted gears. "This is all happening so suddenly, it's hard to know how to feel. But Denise and I are basically looking forward to it, especially now that Max and Deborah are being so great about throwing us the reception and everything."

Callie nodded, though she wondered if Red was really feeling as upbeat as his words indicated. Glancing at the worried set of his brow, she doubted it. He was probably a little scared and a lot uncertain about what was coming. Anyone would be in his situation, Callie supposed. Still, she couldn't seem to focus on that for too long. Her thoughts kept wandering back to Scooby.

"I hope he's okay trailering," she said, thinking aloud. "I don't remember if I asked about that. But Mr. Rayburn said he didn't have any vices. . . ."

"I'm sure he'll be fine," Red said. "From everything you've said, it sounds like your Scooby is a horse with a good head on his shoulders."

They chatted about Scooby and Callie's plans for him for the rest of the short ride. When the tall red barn of Mr. Rayburn's farm came into view, Callie fell silent, gripping the armrest again.

This is it, she thought, suddenly feeling calm. *I'm ready to pick up my horse. My horse.*

It was strange. She'd ridden all sorts of amazing horses, both at Pine Hollow and back in her old hometown. She had even leased one or two. But this would be the first time she would actually own her very own horse.

I guess I never really thought of it that way before, she thought in amazement. *I was so busy trying to figure out which horse would be the best for me that I sort of spaced on the fact that it was actually going to be a horse for* me. *As in* all mine. *Permanently. A real partner.*

Then, for the next few minutes, she didn't have much chance to think at all. Mr. Rayburn was waiting when Red pulled to a stop in front of the barn, and a moment later the farm owner led out Scooby, who was already dressed in shipping bandages. The Appaloosa walked up the ramp like a pro, much to Callie's relief, and stood quietly as she settled him in the trailer.

Callie finally remembered to breathe, inhaling deeply as Red pulled carefully out of the drive and back onto the highway. After giving Mr. Rayburn one last wave, Callie collapsed against her seat. "Whew! Halfway there."

"Right." Red shot her a quick glance and a smile. "Before you know it you'll be bedding him down in his new stall."

Callie smiled. She was always a little nervous when she was shipping a horse, but she managed to distract herself on the ride home by running over everything she wanted to do when they arrived and then planning the next day's ride. Before long they were easing to a stop in front of Pine Hollow. To Callie's surprise, a small crowd was gathered just outside the stable door. She spotted Stevie, Scott, and Lisa right at the front of the crowd. Stevie was holding something, and after squinting at it curiously for a moment, Callie realized that it was a cake.

"What in the world . . . ?" she murmured.

Red grinned as he cut the ignition. "Looks like Scooby's got himself a good old-fashioned Pine Hollow welcoming party."

As soon as Callie hopped out of the truck's cab, Stevie stepped forward. "Surprise!" she cried. "We wanted to make sure Scooby felt welcome right away, so we baked him a cake. A carrot cake, of course!"

"Of course." Callie grinned, a little amazed at the nice gesture. She never would have expected it.

Scott let out a snort. "Baked?" he said. "Try 'bought.'"

"Hey, either way is fine with me," Callie said. "It's the thought that counts. Besides, from the horror stories I've heard about Stevie's cooking, I'm thinking we may be better off this way." She grinned at Stevie to show that she was kidding, then glanced around to see who else had turned out for the occasion. In addition to Stevie, Scott, and Lisa, Denise was there, along with several members of the intermediate riding class. Callie even spotted Ben Marlow hovering in the background.

At that moment Maureen Chance stepped out of the entrance and stopped short in surprise. "What's going on?" she asked. Before anyone could give her an answer, she provided one herself. "Oh! That must be Scooby, right?" She nodded at the trailer.

"Right," Callie said, pleasantly surprised. Though she tended to reserve judgment on new people until she'd known them for a while, Callie hadn't been terribly impressed with Max's new stable hand. While Maureen seemed comfortable and proficient in the way she handled Pine Hollow's horses, she also seemed to have one or two questionable habits. After a lifetime of watching girls approach her handsome, charming brother, Callie was skilled at recognizing incurable flirts, and so far Maureen seemed to be a world-class member of the club.

Of course, that doesn't mean she's not going to make a good stable hand, Callie reminded herself as Maureen walked over to help Red with the trailer. *She seems to be on the ball as far as the horses are concerned.* That was more important than ever now that Callie's horse—her horse!—was going to be under Maureen's care. *Anyway,* she thought, *maybe Maureen's just being a little overfriendly because she's still getting settled. She's just trying to make friends any way she can.*

Callie shot an anxious glance at the trailer behind her, where Red and Maureen were fiddling with the back latch. As much as she was enjoying the impromptu reception, she was eager to get Scooby out of the cramped trailer and into his nice, roomy box stall inside. "Um, so I guess I'd better . . . ," she began uncertainly, not wanting to seem ungrateful for her friends' efforts.

"Right!" Stevie said briskly, obviously guessing exactly what Callie was thinking. She turned to face the small crowd behind her and clapped her hands. "Give her some room! We've got to get this horse inside." Handing the cake to Scott, she gestured toward the door. "Why don't you put this in the locker room? We can eat it once Scooby's settled." As Scott complied, Stevie glanced around at the younger riders. "Anyone who wants to help out could bring down some more hay," she announced. "I'm sure Scooby will be hungry after his trip."

The intermediate students scurried off. Callie blinked in amazement. "Wow. How'd you do that?"

Stevie shrugged. "Oh, I made a few threats before you got here," she said nonchalantly.

Callie wasn't sure if she was kidding or not, but she didn't worry about it too much. It was time to bring Scooby in. "Is he okay?" she asked Red, who was lowering the ramp.

"A-okay," was the reply. "Want to lead him out?"

Callie nodded as Stevie, Lisa, and Denise took a few steps back so that they wouldn't scare the newcomer. Fortunately, Scooby was just as unflappable during unloading as he had been during loading, and Callie soon had him on the ground.

"Wow!" Lisa said, giving the gelding an appreciative once-over. "He's gorgeous!"

Blinking and gazing at the horse, Callie had to agree. Until that point she hadn't really stopped to notice what Scooby looked like, aside from his excellent conformation and alert expression. But now that she thought about it, she realized that he really was impressive-looking, with his all-over leopard pattern, the black spots standing out in sharp contrast to the clean white background. His glossy, healthy coat and well-defined muscles only added to his appeal.

"Thanks," Callie said, giving her horse a pat. "Now come on, I'd better get Mr. Gorgeous inside."

Stevie and Lisa came along to help as Callie led Scooby inside, pausing every so often to let him check out his new surroundings. He sniffed curiously at various items—the lucky horseshoe nailed to the wall near the entrance; Max, who emerged from the indoor ring, where he was teaching a lesson, to see how things were going; and a stray wheelbarrow someone had left tipped up against the wall. But he didn't seem overly concerned or nervous about any of it.

"He's really calm," Stevie commented, sounding impressed.

Callie nodded and smiled, giving Scooby a pat as he walked into his stall with hardly a pause. "Good. He'll have to be, to handle anything unexpected out on the trail."

"Want me to fill his water bucket?" Lisa offered.

Callie nodded gratefully. She had come to the stable early that morning to check the stall and put down a fresh layer of bedding, but there was lots to be done now that the horse was actually there. She was glad that her friends were there to help.

The three of them spent the next few minutes working hard to make Scooby as comfortable as possible. After unwrapping his bandages, Callie grabbed the grooming kit she'd left just outside.

"I'm going to give him a nice grooming now," she said.

Stevie and Lisa nodded. "We'll be around if you need us," Lisa said.

"And don't forget to come out and have some cake later," Stevie reminded her. She grinned. "Don't wait too long, though, or you may miss out. I didn't have much breakfast this morning."

Callie smiled and waved as her friends wandered off down the aisle. As much as she'd enjoyed having them there to help her, she really wanted some time alone with her horse now. She was happy that Stevie and Lisa seemed to understand that without being told.

She was halfway through her pleasant task when she realized she'd misplaced her face brush somehow. "Be right back, buddy," she murmured, giving Scooby a pat and then slipping out of his stall.

This is so great, Callie thought as she hurried toward the tack room in search of a spare. *I can hardly believe how fast it all happened. Just last week, I was wondering if I would ever find a decent horse at all!*

She had reached the hallway across from the stable aisle, and she broke into a jog when the open tack room door came into view. As she rounded the corner, she saw George Wheeler perched on an overturned bucket, scrubbing at a spot on his horse's bridle.

Yikes, Callie thought, skidding to a halt. She hadn't seen much of George for the past week. Not only had he been staying out of her way at school, but he always seemed to disappear whenever she turned up at Pine Hollow as well. She was glad that he was finally honoring their arrangement. It was about time.

Still, there was no reason she couldn't be civil. "Hello," she said calmly as she headed for the tack trunk near the stack of saddle pads in one corner.

George cleared his throat. "Um, hi," he said in a subdued voice. "Congratulations on your new horse."

"Thanks." Callie wasn't sure what else to say. Hiding her self-consciousness by bending and digging through the trunk, she quickly found what she needed. Then, brush in hand, she hovered in the doorway for a moment, feeling guilty about the melancholy expression on George's pudgy, red-cheeked face. But he had already returned his attention to his task and didn't seem inclined to further conversation, so, after an awkward few seconds, Callie escaped once again through the door.

She hurried down the hallway. That had been a decidedly uncomfortable encounter—much worse than seeing him at school, where there were always lots of other people around.

Oh well, she thought with a mental shrug. *I guess it will take both of us some time to adjust to our new arrangement. That's only natural. I'm sure after a while we won't even remember how weird things are between us.*

She turned the corner and saw Scooby's head hanging out over the half door. He was looking her way. She smiled. Luckily, she had plenty to distract her in the meantime.

Stevie was in a good mood when she arrived home from the stable. She loved it when new horses came to Pine Hollow, whether they were school horses or were privately owned. It was even nicer to see a good friend bring home a wonderful, well-matched horse, and Callie and Scooby definitely fit that bill.

She was whistling when she walked into the kitchen and tossed her car keys in the bowl near the refrigerator and her parka over a chair. Her twin brother was sitting at the counter reading a magazine and eating a bowl of cereal, which he'd managed to slop all over the otherwise clean surface. "What are you so chipper about?" he asked, glancing up at her.

"Life," Stevie replied succinctly.

Alex rolled his eyes. "Does this mean you're still all full of yourself because of that article?"

Stevie grinned. "Are you jealous?" she teased.

Alex snorted. "Yeah, right," he said sarcastically.

"By the way, Phil called. The message is on the machine."

"Thanks." Stevie hurried over to the answering machine and pressed the button.

"Hi, it's Phil calling for Stevie," her boyfriend's familiar voice came out of the tiny speaker. *"Stevie, I'm on my way out to see my sister's play, but I wanted to let you know that A.J. called just now. He finally got a lead on that woman in the picture, and so today he tracked down her name and number and left a message on her answering machine. Thought you'd like to know!"*

"Wow!" Stevie exclaimed as the message ended. She glanced at her brother. "Did you hear that? This is amazing!"

Alex nodded. "It's pretty cool," he agreed. "Maybe this will help A.J. pull things together. It's about time." He cleared his throat and stirred his cereal with his spoon. "By the way, did I hear Phil say something about being busy tonight? I guess that means you aren't going to argue when I remind you it's my turn for the car."

"What?" Stevie frowned. "No way. I need it tonight. I'm going to the movies with Lisa and Callie." The three of them had arranged the outing before Stevie had left the stable. It had been tough to convince Callie to agree, since she seemed ready to move right into Scooby's stall. Not that Stevie blamed her. She knew how it felt to have a wonderful new horse and want to spend every minute with him or her. Still, as she had reminded Callie, even wonderful new horses had to sleep. "I already offered to drive."

"Too bad." Alex dropped his spoon and frowned. "I need the car, too. And like I said, it's my turn."

Stevie pursed her lips in annoyance. She couldn't really argue the last point—after all, she'd had the car at Pine Hollow all afternoon, leaving Alex to find his own way home from school. Still, he might have given her a little more warning if he was going to grab it away from her now. "What do you need it for?" she demanded.

"I have a date." From the slightly defiant expression on his face, Stevie didn't even have to ask who her brother was seeing that evening. It had to be Nicole Adams.

She gritted her teeth, trying to hold back all of the comments she wanted to make. The last thing she wanted was to get into another argument with Alex about Nicole. "Can't you ask your *date* to drive, then?" she asked. "She does know how, doesn't she? Or is there, like, a minimum IQ requirement to get your license now?"

"Hello?" a voice called from the front hall, interrupting the tense moment. "Anybody home?"

Stevie blinked in surprise. "Is that Chad?"

"Sounds like," Alex said. "What's he doing here? I thought he wasn't coming home until Monday after his last exam."

Before Stevie could answer, her older brother loped into the kitchen. Chad was a sophomore at NVU, and he tended to dress like a complete stereotype of a college student, especially during exams. That day, for instance, he was wearing unlaced high-tops without socks, a red NVU sweatshirt, and purple sweatpants with a large, fraying hole in one knee and a dark stain of indeterminate origin covering much of the opposite leg.

"Yo!" Chad said when he saw them. "Merry Christmas, kiddos!"

"Back at ya," Stevie responded. "What are you doing here?"

Chad feigned hurt. "What do you mean? Aren't you happy to see your favorite big brother?"

"We thought you had finals," Alex said. "Mom and Dad said you wouldn't be home until Monday night."

"I managed to move my econ exam up," Chad explained. "I finished it an hour ago. So here I am!" He straddled a chair and grabbed an apple out of the bowl in the middle of the kitchen table. Taking a big bite, he looked from one twin to the other. "So," he said through a mouthful of apple, "what are you two up to now that Christmas break is finally here?"

"Not much," Stevie muttered. "Especially since Alex is hogging the car."

"Oh, please." Alex shot her a dirty look. "Just because I happen to want to use *my* car when it's *my* turn—"

"Whoa, whoa." Chad lowered his apple. "Is that any way to show your holiday spirit? Now, I think you two had better kiss and make up. You're, like, totally harshing my holiday vibe, dudes." He grinned and took another big bite of the apple.

"Whatever," Alex muttered, bending over his cereal.

Chad raised an eyebrow. "What's with him?" he asked Stevie.

Stevie scowled at Alex as she addressed Chad. "Don't ask me," she said. "But as for kissing and making up, forget it. My whole night's plans are screwed up just because he suddenly announces that he's taking out Nicole Adams tonight."

"Really?" Chad let out a low whistle and turned to stare at Alex. "Are you talking about the same Nicole Adams I'm remembering? She was, like, the hottest girl in school my senior year, even though she was only a freshman. Since when do you go for that flavor, little brother?"

Alex looked slightly embarrassed. "Nicole's nice," he said defensively. "Anyway, we're just hanging out. It's no big deal."

"Whatever." Chad shrugged. "I'm just saying."

Stevie couldn't help feeling a twinge of annoyance at Chad. Why was he making such a big deal about Nicole? What better girlfriend could Alex ask for than Lisa?

She tried not to let her feelings show. Chad was just being his usual girl-crazy self, after all—he couldn't be expected to appreciate stuff like true love and commitment. Not unless he'd suddenly evolved a whole lot more that semester, which would practically be a miracle as far as Stevie was concerned.

Chad took one last bite of his apple, then stood and tossed the core into the trash can near the back door. "What about you, Stevie? What's new? You didn't ditch Phil for Mr. Universe or anything, did you?"

"Very funny." Stevie wrinkled her nose. Even though Chad was being sort of obnoxious, she had to admit he still made her laugh. It was nice having him home again, even if he was only staying a couple of weeks. "Hey, by the way, what are you doing tonight? Want to come to the movies? Lisa and Callie and I are catching a show over at the mall. You can talk to Lisa about NVU. Did I tell you she's going there next year?"

Chad blinked in surprise but then nodded. "Sure, why not?" He shrugged. "I guess that could be fun.

I haven't seen Lisa since your party. And your friend Callie seems pretty cool."

"Great! Then you can drive." Stevie grinned at her older brother.

There! she thought with satisfaction. *Talk about killing two birds with one stone! Not only do we have a ride, but this will give me the perfect opportunity to hit up Chad for that cash Christmas gift. I'm sure he'll be just as thrilled as Michael and Alex were to have an excuse to skip the mall this year.*

"Uh-huh, sure thing, Stevie," Chad replied absently. His curious gaze was fixed on Alex once again. "So seriously, give me the four-one-one, baby bro," he said, leaning over to punch Alex in the shoulder. "How did a goober like you manage to hook up with a hottie like Nicole Adams, anyway? Was it threats? Hypnotism?"

Stevie sighed, her sunny mood slipping just a bit. *When is Alex going to wake up and realize he's wasting his time with bimbo Nicole?* she wondered with a slight frown, suddenly glad that Scott had other plans and wouldn't be joining them that night. *When is he going to get a clue and start begging Lisa to take him back—before it's too late?*

10
TEN

Callie fought back a yawn as she stepped into Pine Hollow's entryway the next morning. *I can't believe how late I went to bed last night,* she thought ruefully. *And I'm paying for it now. What was I thinking?*

Going to the movies had seemed like a good idea at the time, especially since she wanted to give Scooby time to settle in and relax rather than having to put up with her staying at Pine Hollow all night, as she was tempted to do. And she had definitely enjoyed herself. She'd been kind of surprised when Chad Lake had tagged along—she'd been expecting a girls' night out. But Chad had ended up being a lot of fun, whispering funny comments to Callie and the others during the movie, which had been completely lame, and tossing popcorn into Stevie's hair whenever her back was turned. When Chad had suggested a postmovie pit stop at their favorite burger place, that had seemed like a pretty good idea, too. After that, Callie had lost track of the time. She had been having a great time laughing until her sides hurt at Chad's goofy jokes, and before she knew it the quick snack had somehow turned into a three-hour marathon of talking, eating, goofing around, and generally hanging out. When Stevie had reluctantly pointed out that it was nearly midnight—the younger Lakes' weekend curfew—Callie had been amazed. Not to mention dismayed.

It's ironic, she thought as she glanced around the quiet entryway. *Here I am getting ready to start working on Scooby's attention and discipline, among other things, and I seem to have totally lost both qualities myself.*

Yawning again, she made a quick stop in the locker room to pick up her gloves and boots, then headed toward Scooby's stall. Tired or not, she had a full schedule in mind for that day. First on the agenda was spending some serious time with Scooby in the schooling ring, figuring out exactly what she had to work with so that she could plan their training.

The Appaloosa was nosing at his hayrack when Callie looked over the half door, but he immediately turned to face her. "Hey, buddy," Callie called softly as the horse stepped toward her with his ears pricked forward. "How was your first night in your new home?"

Judging by the look of the horse, it had gone just fine. Callie was happy to see that Scooby looked calm, happy, and well rested. Not only did that bode well for that day's exercise, but it also meant he would probably be fine if they needed to travel and stay in strange barns for competitions.

After giving him a quick grooming, Callie went to get her tack. She had been using her old endurance saddle on Barq, and the day before she'd tested it on Scooby just long enough to see if it would fit him. It did, though she'd had to borrow a slightly longer girth from Max.

"Okay, boy," she announced as she returned to Scooby's stall. "Ready to really get acquainted?"

Scooby stood quietly as she tacked him up, shifting his feet uneasily only when she tightened the girth. He took the bit with no hesitation, and before long he was ready to go.

Callie led him outside and mounted. Then she walked him around the ring for a few minutes to warm him up. He kept his ears swiveling curiously as he walked, seeming to enjoy the meager winter sunshine and even the slight breeze blowing in from the fields, though Callie herself found it rather chilly on her face. When she finally asked for a trot, Scooby swung right into the two-beat gait, maintaining a steady rhythm until halfway around the ring, when she asked for another change. Once again he responded to her aids immediately. His extended trot was smooth and easy, covering more ground than Callie expected, even after her previous rides on him.

"Wow," Callie murmured, impressed anew with the horse's proficiency. "Somebody trained you but good, bud."

Scooby's ears flicked back alertly at the sound of her voice, but he didn't break stride. Callie steadied him, then asked for a canter. He swung into it handily, and Callie smiled. *So far, so good,* she thought. As happy as she was with her new horse, a tiny, pessimistic part of her kept looking for something wrong with him. *I can't really be this lucky, can I?* she wondered as she easily shifted the horse back down to a trot.

Callie was so focused on what she was doing that Scooby noticed Ben Marlow's arrival before she did. The gelding was trotting along calmly when he suddenly snorted and took a step sideways.

"Ho!" Callie said, quickly collecting her mount again as she caught a glimpse of a person approaching the ring's fence. Fortunately, Scooby didn't really seem frightened, and he returned almost immediately to his previous steady pace. Callie wasn't sure his action even qualified as a spook—more of a break of stride. When she was sure that Scooby wasn't going to react further, she glanced over at the fence. Ben raised a hand to her.

"Sorry," he called. "He okay?"

"He's fine." Callie brought Scooby to a walk, then bent forward to pat his shoulder. She turned him toward Ben, riding toward the fence so that she could speak to him without shouting. She and Ben weren't exactly close—in fact, she couldn't remember the last time they'd spoken more than a few words to each other—but Callie knew that the taciturn stable hand really knew his stuff when it came to horses. She was curious how he would react to Scooby.

Ben was leaning on the top rail of the schooling ring, watching Scooby intently. The horse returned his look curiously, stretching his head toward him. Ben reached out to stroke the gelding's face, his own face softening into a half smile.

"How does he look?" Callie asked.

Ben didn't look up at her as he replied, instead keeping his gaze trained steadily on the horse as he rubbed Scooby's face and neck. "Good. Nice movement. Seems well trained."

Callie grinned. From Ben, that surely qualified as a glowing approval speech. "Thanks," she said. "I just hope he's as good out on the trail as he is in the ring. What did you think of our shoulder-in?"

Ben started to say something about Scooby's hip movement, but Callie missed the majority of his response. A flash of movement at the stable entrance had caught her eye, and a second later she saw George leading his horse, Joyride, into the yard. He led the mare to the mounting block and swung into the saddle, not so much as glancing in Callie's direction, though she was sure he knew she was there.

What's that about? she thought, feeling a familiar stab of guilt as George gathered his reins and clucked to his mare. He was close enough to the ring that the sound carried to Callie. *I know I told him to stay away from me, but it's like he's pretending I don't exist or something.*

That didn't bother her too much, but the sight of George's pudgy figure riding out of the yard alone did disturb her a little. He just looked so pathetic, so lonely. . . . She kept her eyes on him until he'd reached the big south pasture and passed through the gate, closing it carefully behind him.

Then Callie shook her head and turned back to Ben, wondering what was wrong with her. Why was she sitting there obsessing over George's state of mind and his emotional health? Whatever he might be feeling about her now, it was all for the best in the long run. He had finally gotten the hint, and that was what she wanted.

She smiled apologetically at Ben, vowing to put

George out of her mind for good. "Sorry," she said to Ben. "What was that again?"

Lisa blinked as Scott led her past yet another set of theater doors. "Where are these seats anyway, on the stage?" she joked.

Scott glanced over at her and smiled. "We're almost there. I think you'll like them."

"Okay." Lisa wasn't about to argue. She had never been in this particular section of the theater, though she'd seen a variety of productions there over the years. Usually when she was paying for tickets to a play or concert herself, she went for the cheap seats in the second balcony. Years earlier, when her parents had taken her to see children's concerts and other things, they had usually ended up in the aptly named family circle.

Soon they reached yet another pair of propped-open doors. Scott held out their ticket stubs to the portly woman standing guard, and she gave them a quick glance. "Come this way, please," the woman said, already turning to lead the way down the plush, carpeted aisle.

Lisa's eyes widened as she realized they were in the very front section. *Wow,* she thought with a tingle of excitement. *I guess this is one of the fringe benefits of hanging out with a congressman's son.*

The usher led them to the third row and gestured

to the two seats on the end. "Thank you," Scott said politely. Then he turned to Lisa. "Would you like the inside seat or the aisle?"

"I don't care," Lisa said, a little overwhelmed as she glanced around. For a moment she felt under-dressed—she had chosen her outfit carefully, but it couldn't compare to the mink stole on the woman directly behind her or the sparkly evening gown on the woman across the aisle. Then she spotted an eld-erly woman dressed in an expensive-looking but ca-sual pantsuit, as well as a young couple wearing jeans, sitting in the row in front of her, and she relaxed.

Soon she and Scott were seated and flipping through their programs. As they chatted about the dancers' previous credits and about other topics, Lisa lost her last bit of self-consciousness about be-ing there. It was amazing how sitting with Scott in the high-priced seats of a fancy big-city theater felt just as comfortable as sitting across the table from him at the local pizza place or talking with him in the locker room at Pine Hollow. Soon she had al-most forgotten where they were.

She remembered again when the overture began and the dancers took the stage. "Wow!" she whis-pered to Scott. "I can actually see the whites of their eyes from here. I always thought that was just an expression."

Scott smiled in response. Then they both turned to watch the performance.

The production was excellent, though for a while Lisa had a little trouble focusing on the action on-stage. She'd seen *The Nutcracker* many times before, but this time felt totally different. For one thing, thanks to their fantastic seats, it felt as if they were practically in the dancers' laps. For another, Lisa found herself very aware of Scott sitting in the seat beside her, even though she kept her eyes directed toward the stage. The faint scent of his aftershave tickled her nose, and she was hyperaware of his arm almost touching hers on the armrest between them.

This is nice, she thought, sneaking a quick glance at Scott between scenes. *This is really nice.*

She was a little surprised at what a good time she was having. Over the past couple of days, she had just about convinced herself that her first date with Scott had been a fluke—a sort of sample date to test whether she could really have a good time without Alex by her side. She was starting to realize that the answer to that question was yes, though she wasn't sure whether or not Scott himself was a major part of the reason.

Maybe it's just the first-class treatment going to my head, she thought. *I mean, it's awfully nice to have a good-looking, popular guy like Scott making such an effort to show me a good time. It's been a while since*

anyone other than Alex has shown this much interest.
So maybe I'm just feeling really flattered right now.

The dancers took their places again, and Lisa did her best to stop worrying about it. She would figure it out later. For now, she just wanted to relax and enjoy the show.

Stevie was carefully applying a thin coat of mascara to her sandy blond eyelashes when Chad walked by the open door of her room and poked his head in. "Hey, thought you had some hot date tonight," he commented with a grin. "Aren't you going to clean yourself up and put on some decent clothes?"

"Ha, ha," Stevie said, making a face at him in the mirror. Capping her mascara, she turned around and checked the alarm clock on her bedside table. "As a matter of fact, I'm leaving in fifteen minutes to meet Phil."

"Cool." Chad lounged in the doorway. "By the way, thanks for inviting me last night. It was fun."

Stevie smiled. "Yeah. It was." She had actually been a little surprised at the way Chad had fit in with her friends. He and Lisa had always been more than cordial with each other—well, since the time when Chad was fourteen and decided he had a crush on her, anyway—but Stevie hadn't been too certain that her brother and Callie would hit it off.

Callie could be really serious and intense sometimes, and Chad was pretty much the opposite of that. But things had gone smoothly right from the start, and Stevie was pretty sure that all of them had ended up having a great time.

Chad moved on, and Stevie gave herself one last satisfied glance in the mirror. She was really looking forward to her date with Phil that night. He'd called a little earlier to confirm and mentioned that A.J. still hadn't had any response to the message he'd left the mysterious woman who might be his mother. Stevie was disappointed about that, but she figured that if A.J. could be patient, so could she. And going out and having fun with Phil seemed like a sure way to take her mind off just about everything else.

As Stevie headed for the door, her gaze fell on the shopping bag on the floor near her closet. She couldn't resist going to it and pulling out the large red-and-white box inside.

It was totally worth skipping out early on Belle and fighting my way through the mall today, she thought with satisfaction as she set the box on her bed and lifted off the top. As many times as she looked at the thick folds of supple leather inside, she never got tired of checking out the chaps. *Of course, it would have been nice if they'd had his size in stock,* she added with a flash of irritation. *There's no way he's going to fit into these—they're more like my size than his.*

She hadn't been able to resist buying the too-small pair, though, especially when the sales clerk had assured her that Phil would have no trouble at all exchanging them for the correct size after Christmas. The chaps were even more beautiful than she'd remembered, and she knew that Phil was going to be thrilled with them. She just couldn't bear to settle for a gift certificate instead.

Anyway, this means he can even pick out the color he wants without worrying about hurting my feelings, she thought, remembering that the chaps came in black and tan as well as the dark brown she'd chosen. She ran her hand over the chocolate-colored leather one last time before carefully replacing the lid. *Of course, if you ask me, this color is pretty much perfect.*

Scott's hand felt warm as it held Lisa's tightly. The two of them were strolling up Lisa's front walk. It was late—the ballet hadn't ended until after ten, and then there had been the forty-minute drive back to Willow Creek—and the neighborhood was dark and peaceful, with only a few scattered lights showing in houses up and down the block. A few doors down, the Lakes' garage light burned brightly, a sure sign that either Alex or Stevie, if not both, was still out.

Lisa glanced ahead at her own dark house. Obviously her mother had forgotten to leave the porch light on for her as she usually did. Trying not to let thoughts of her mother intrude on her pleasant mood, she cleared her throat and glanced up at Scott. "Thanks again for tonight," she said. "I had a really nice time."

"Me too." Scott returned her smile, squeezing her hand slightly. "Did you really have fun?"

"Absolutely." Lisa meant it, too. In fact, she couldn't remember the last time she'd had such a pleasant evening. Probably not since before she'd sent back that college acceptance, or since she and Alex had started having problems. She pushed that last thought out of her mind as quickly as it came. This wasn't the time to start thinking about Alex. She cleared her throat and smiled at Scott. "Thanks again."

"Any time." Scott stopped as they reached the porch and turned to face her, taking both her hands in his own. "Does this mean you'll go on the Starlight Ride with me next week?"

Lisa hesitated, wondering how to respond to that. Yes, it was true that she'd had a great time with Scott that evening—much better than she had expected. Still, she really didn't know what she felt for him. Was he just a good friend? Could he ever be anything more? She just didn't think she could decide at the moment, especially while things remained unre-

147

solved with Alex. And she didn't want to lead Scott on, make him think they were going to be together if it wasn't going to happen.

"I—I don't know," she said uncertainly, realizing that Scott was waiting for her answer. "That is, it sounds like fun, but I really don't know if it's a good idea. I need to think about it. See, things are just so weird for me right now, with Alex and—and—well, everything. And I don't want things to move too fast, because, um, I'm not sure where they're going. Where I want them to go, I mean. Do you know what I mean?"

She winced in anticipation of his response, hoping that he wouldn't be too hurt by her direct words. She could only imagine what Alex would say if he were in Scott's place at that moment. He would probably take it totally personally, give her that sad-puppy look of his, and then slink off to nurse his wounds in private.

But Scott didn't seem upset at all. He nodded. "I understand," he said softly. "But think about it, okay? The offer stands. No pressure."

Lisa blinked. Before she could get over her surprise at his mild reaction, Scott leaned down and kissed her.

The touch of his lips on hers was like an electric shock that set her heart pounding a mile a minute. Each time they kissed, her reaction seemed to get stronger. *What does this mean?* she thought, her head spinning out of control as she melted into Scott's embrace. *Why should a simple kiss have this effect on me—like I've never been kissed before?*

Before she could figure it out, Scott pulled away. "Good night, Lisa," he murmured, gently pushing a strand of blond hair off her cheek before stepping back. "I'll see you tomorrow."

"Uh, y-yeah," Lisa stammered, unable to come up with a more intelligent response. Swallowing hard and wiping her suddenly sweaty palms on her jacket, she turned and raced into the dark house without looking back.

ELEVEN

Callie was at Pine Hollow early again on Sunday. She headed for the schooling ring, hoping to get in some solid time before Max's first private lesson a little later that morning. "Ready to get started, buddy?" she asked, patting Scooby soundly on the neck before bending over to adjust her left stirrup.

Scooby stood quietly until she was ready, then stepped forward smartly at her first light squeeze. Callie spent a few minutes warming him up, then moved on to some exercises she'd planned, working on some serpentines and figure eights and then trotting over a row of cavalletti.

Once again, the schooling session went very well. Scooby did just about everything she asked right away. While she could tell that they were going to have to work on a few things, it was nothing she couldn't handle. Callie was already starting to think of herself and Scooby as a team, and she liked the feeling. She liked it a lot.

She was just thinking, reluctantly, that it was time to head in and let Scooby rest when she noticed that Ben Marlow had stopped by to watch again on his way back from the grain shed with a bag of feed. Remembering how helpful—and uncharacteristically talkative—he'd been the previous day, Callie stopped what she was doing and rode toward him, eager to take advantage of any new comments he might have about Scooby.

"Hey," she greeted him as she brought Scooby to a halt. "How do we look today?"

As usual, Ben didn't waste time on formalities. "Check your right side," he said. "Looks like you're still favoring it a little."

Callie glanced down at her right leg, the one that had been injured in the accident and had kept her from endurance riding for so long. Though it had recovered fully, she realized that Ben might be right—she might still be automatically adjusting for its previous weakness.

"Thanks," she said, readjusting her position slightly.

Ben nodded. Then his attention turned to Callie's horse. "Scooby looks great. Happy with him so far?"

"Definitely." Callie smiled and leaned forward to

pat her horse fondly. "He's doing terrific. Of course, we haven't really been out in the woods together," she added, her smile fading slightly. "The closest we came was a little trail around the pasture at Mr. Rayburn's farm. And Mr. Rayburn said Scooby can be a little headstrong on the trail, especially when he's feeling fresh." That was the one thing that had been worrying her a little. She didn't mind a horse who had a mind of his own and wasn't afraid to show it, but a truly headstrong mount would be a constant struggle, and that could eat up a lot more energy than a good endurance team could afford. "I just hope a little early energy is all it is," she muttered, more to herself than to Ben. She trusted Mr. Rayburn's word—she wouldn't have bought Scooby if she didn't—but she knew that the farmer wasn't an endurance expert. What might seem "a little fresh" to him might seem irretrievably headstrong to her, especially during a race.

Ben shrugged. "Easy answer," he said. "Take him out and see."

Callie blinked, realizing that he was right. Here she was, spending two full days schooling in the ring when she hadn't even fully tested her horse yet in the environment where they would eventually be spending most of their time—the trail. "Of course," she said slowly, feeling a bit foolish. "That makes sense.

I'll take him out tomorrow." She smiled at Ben. "Thanks for pointing out the obvious."

Ben shrugged again. "Stuff that should be obvious isn't always."

He turned away and hoisted his bag of feed before Callie could respond further. She watched him walk off into the stable, a little amazed, as she always was, at the way he could be so helpful and insightful once in a while and yet so taciturn and almost sullen the rest of the time.

Then she forgot about Ben and returned her attention to Scooby. "Ready for a nice relaxing grooming?" she asked him cheerfully. She was already looking forward to the next day's ride, though a tiny knot of nervousness had settled into the pit of her stomach. She knew it wouldn't dissipate until she'd tested Scooby on the trail.

After dismounting, she led Scooby out of the ring. They were heading for the stable entrance when she saw Carole's familiar red junker pull in. Carole caught up to them a moment later just outside the door.

"Hi!" Carole said breathlessly, stepping forward to let Scooby sniff her. "This must be Scooby."

"It sure is." Callie grinned proudly as Carole patted and scratched the horse, looking him over from stem to stern.

"He's gorgeous! Sorry I couldn't be here for the welcome party." Carole smiled sheepishly at Callie as she gave the horse a rub under his chin. "It's easy to use up my stable time these days without even realizing it, and by Friday I was all out. I've been dying to see him, but I couldn't come yesterday either because I was out with my dad all day."

"It's okay. I understand." Callie knew that the rules of Carole's grounding allowed her only four visits to Pine Hollow per week, and that those visits could be only two hours long. For a horse-crazy girl like Carole, that had to be the next best thing to torture. Callie knew that she would have trouble limiting herself like that. It had been bad enough after her accident, when her riding had been constrained by her own physical condition. "At least New Year's is only a little over a week away now."

"I know. I'm counting the days." Carole checked her watch and grimaced. "Meanwhile, though, I have to count the minutes. If I want to get anything done today, I should get moving."

"Me too." Callie clucked to Scooby, and all three of them headed into the building. "I want to get Scooby settled in for the day—we're going to hit the trails tomorrow, and he'll need his rest."

"Really? Where are you going to go?"

Callie shrugged. "I'm not sure yet exactly, but if everything goes well in the beginning of our ride, I'll probably try to head into the state forest and find some challenging spots to test him out."

Carole smiled and patted Scooby on the shoulder. "That sounds great. I'm sure you'll both enjoy it. Have fun."

"Thanks. Have fun today with Starlight."

"I will." Carole waved as Callie headed across the entryway toward the stable aisle with Scooby in tow. Then she turned the other way, toward the tack room. She was happy for Callie—she always loved seeing a rider matched with a compatible horse—but at the moment she had to admit that she was much more interested in her own problem. She just couldn't seem to come up with a good idea for Cam's Christmas gift. She still wanted to find something that would be truly meaningful, and after the poetry fiasco, she had considered several other possibilities, from baking him a cake to knitting him a sweater. But a cake didn't seem special enough, and Carole seriously doubted she could learn to knit well enough in the next week to make anything decent. Nothing else she thought of seemed right, either.

She was thinking hard when she wandered into the tack room and saw George Wheeler. He was hanging up his horse's bridle on its assigned bracket, and as he stretched, his tight wool sweater crept up a bit in back to expose a sliver of pale skin.

Carole averted her eyes from the less-than-lovely

sight and cleared her throat. "Hi, George," she said politely. She had never gotten to know George very well, even though he had been riding at Pine Hollow almost daily for the past year and a half. He had always been a little shy, and with all the work and activity of the stable, Carole just hadn't had time to get past that and find out what he was all about. The only thing she really knew about him, aside from the fact that he'd had a crush on Callie for months, was that he was an excellent rider. As unlikely as it seemed for a guy with his personality and body type, he had won more than his share of ribbons in eventing.

"Hi, Carole," George responded in his soft, tentative voice. "Going for a ride?"

"Uh-huh." Carole smile at him and then walked over to grab Starlight's bridle. She was expecting George to move on, since he seemed to be finishing up, and was a bit startled when she turned around and saw him standing in the middle of the room, watching her with his arms tucked behind his back. Carole smiled again, a little uncertainly this time. "Um, I figured I'd take Starlight out for a hack, since it's not too cold today."

"That sounds nice." George smiled, still standing there watching her.

Carole slung her bridle over one shoulder and then turned to hoist Starlight's saddle off its rack.

She wasn't sure why George was hanging around, and it was making her a bit uncomfortable. "Anyway," she said blankly, searching for something to fill the silence, "Starlight has always loved the trails. I love trail riding, too. It was one of the first things I learned to love about riding, just heading into the woods and having fun. I mean, I'm not Callie or anything—Starlight and I aren't going to be jaunting off into the depths of the state forest like she and Scooby are doing tomorrow." She laughed weakly, wondering why she couldn't seem to stop babbling. George's bland, silent stare was making her much too nervous. As she grabbed for Starlight's girth, it slipped out of her fingers and slithered to the floor. Bending over to fish it out from under a saddle rack, she clamped her mouth shut and vowed to get a grip. Still, she wished George would just go away already so that she could go back to thinking about Cam.

"Um, I'd better go," George said at that moment, as if reading her thoughts.

Carole stood up quickly and turned around, hoping she hadn't inadvertently let him know what she was feeling. She might not be thrilled about hanging around the tack room chatting with George, but she didn't want to be rude.

As she turned, she quickly realized the reason for George's hasty departure. Ben Marlow was standing in the doorway holding an empty box of deworming paste.

Carole gulped. She hadn't seen much of Ben lately, and his appearance caught her off guard. "Um, hi," she said as George slipped out past Ben.

Ben merely nodded in response, then headed over to the medicine cabinet above the sink. Swinging open the door, he rummaged around inside without a word.

Carole stood clutching her tack, wondering why her feet suddenly seemed to be frozen to the floor. While George's presence had made her tongue run nonstop, Ben's sudden appearance was having the opposite effect. Her mind felt dull and slow, and she couldn't seem to come up with one single thing to say to him.

Finally she managed to collect her thoughts enough to blurt out, "What are you looking for?"

Ben glanced at her over his shoulder. "Dewormer," he said. "Checkers just knocked his in his water bucket, so Maureen needs another tube."

"Oh." Carole winced slightly at the new stable hand's name. She still wasn't sure if her reaction had anything to do with the young woman herself or if it was just sour grapes because she couldn't quite get over the idea that Maureen had taken over the job that should by all rights still belong to Carole. "Maureen. Um, so how's she working out?"

Ben shrugged. "She knows horses."

He didn't seem inclined to elaborate. "Um, that's good," Carole said lamely. She couldn't help thinking that, as usual, Ben didn't seem eager to chat with her. Still, she couldn't quite bring herself to leave the room with Starlight's tack. Instead she puttered around, first fiddling with the girth and then leaning over a bucket of spare stirrup leathers and pretending to search for one.

Ben remained silent as he dropped his empty dewormer in the wastebasket and headed for the door with the full one. For a moment Carole thought he was going to leave without the two of them exchanging another word. But he paused in the doorway and half turned toward her. "Uh, bye," he muttered.

Carole was so startled that it took her a moment to respond. "See you later!" she called finally, though she wasn't sure whether he heard her or not, since he had already disappeared around the corner.

How does he always manage to do that to me? Why do I always seem to turn into a blithering idiot when he's in the room? she wondered. She had been trying to figure out Ben since she'd met him more than two years earlier and was really no closer to doing so than she'd ever been.

With a sigh, she tried to return her thoughts to Cam as she left the room with her tack and walked down the hall, heading for Starlight's stall. The more time passed, the more anxious she got about finding the perfect gift to demonstrate how she felt about him. But somehow, her mind couldn't quite seem to let go of the awkward little encounter with Ben.

If I were shopping for him instead, this would be easy. The thought sprang into her head unbidden. *I could just go to The Saddlery and pick out something I loved myself and be pretty sure he would love it, too.*

She frowned, her steps slowing as she turned down the aisle toward Starlight's stall. Where had that idea come from? She had no idea what sort of Christmas gift Ben would like.

But she knew that wasn't really true. Like her, Ben lived, breathed, slept, and dreamed horses. If she bought him a manure fork or a new grooming kit, he would love it. If she got him those chaps that Stevie was giving Phil, Ben would love that, too. If she offered him half ownership of Starlight as her gift, he would be even more thrilled—not that he would show it, but she knew it would be true nonetheless.

"Hey, buddy," she said, interrupting her own thoughts as Starlight came to the front of his stall to meet her. "Ready to go?"

Starlight didn't respond except to butt at her gently with his head, but Carole could tell that the gelding was feeling frisky. That was good. Thinking about guys—Ben, and even Cam—was starting to make her head hurt. She figured she might as well take her mind off both of them, and everything else, by throwing herself into the one activity that had always been able to absorb her completely. Maybe the real physical exercise and simple emotional satisfaction of riding would give her some perspective on everything else.

I'm really glad there's no school today, Callie thought with satisfaction, taking a deep breath of the hay-and-horse-scented air as she entered Pine Hollow the next morning. *It's definitely the best early Christmas present I could ask for. Because I don't think I could sit through six and a half hours of classes before I took Scooby out on the trails. Not when I'm dying to know if this partnership is going to work out.*

She had spent most of the previous evening thinking about her future with Scooby, and as far as she could remember, she'd also spent much of the night dreaming about the same topic. Now it was time to find out once and for all if she'd made the right choice.

When she walked into the office, the first thing that met her eyes was the bottom of Maureen's well-worn paddock boots, which were propped up on Max's desk. The new stable hand was leaning back in the desk chair, a mug in one hand and the other hand resting between her head and the wall behind her. Red was leaning against the edge of the desk, a chipped cup propped on his knee. From what Callie heard, the two of them seemed to be discussing a TV show they'd both seen the night before. The distinctive smell of coffee permeated the small room.

Callie cleared her throat, since neither of the adults noticed her standing there. "Good morning."

"Oh, hi, Callie." Red turned and smiled at her. "Want a cuppa?"

"No thanks. I just stopped in to let you know that I'm planning to hit the trails today," she said, trying not to notice that Maureen's leg was almost touching Red's jeans. "I expect to leave as soon as I can get Scooby tacked, and if all goes well, I'll be back around two."

Maureen blinked, seeming confused at the information, but Red nodded and grabbed a pen and notepad. "Okay," he said. "What's your intended route?"

"I'm not completely sure," she said. "I want to search out some interesting footing, so it will sort of depend on what I find along the way. But I can draw you a rough map of the major possibilities. And I'm taking my cell phone along in case there are any big changes." She patted her bulging jacket pocket, where she'd stashed the tiny phone along with a foil-wrapped sandwich and some other items that she planned to transfer into a cantle bag for the ride.

"Okay." Red handed over the pen and paper.

Callie quickly sketched out the route she had in mind. She had a pretty good idea of where she wanted to go, based on her experiences riding Barq and other horses.

"That's an awfully long trail ride," Maureen commented, swinging her feet down to the floor and leaning forward to see the notepad. "Anyway, why are you telling us where you're going to be riding?"

"Callie's an endurance rider," Red explained. "She'll be out alone today, and we need to know where to look if she doesn't make it back when she's supposed to."

Maureen gave Callie a slow, appraising glance. "Endurance, huh? Interesting. But I thought the kids weren't allowed to ride solo off the property."

Callie flinched at the word *kids*—after all, Maureen wasn't all *that* much older than she was. "The *younger* kids aren't allowed out alone," she said, keeping a lid on her temper. Maureen was new, after all. She couldn't possibly know all the ins and outs of Pine Hollow's rules yet. "But Max lets the more advanced riders like me go out by themselves."

"Not that he's crazy about that, either," Red interjected. "But as long as we have as much information as humanly possible, he can live with it."

Maureen rolled her eyes and laughed. "Yeah, I could see him giving himself an ulcer over something like that. Max is pretty cool, but he's kind of uptight about some stuff."

Callie thought that was a little harsh—Max had to be responsible if he wanted to successfully manage thirty-odd horses, not to mention an even greater number of riders encompassing everything from rank beginners to seasoned competitors. But she definitely didn't feel like standing around debating it. "Okay, then," she said briskly, already moving toward the door. "I'd better get going. See you this afternoon."

Callie patted Scooby on the withers as she kicked her feet out of the stirrups and prepared to dismount. "Good job so far, boy," she said, not bothering to disguise the pride in her voice. "Excellent job, in fact. Maybe it's true, you are a little headstrong, but so am I. So we're going to do just fine."

She could hardly contain the relief she felt. After just an hour on the trail, she was already certain that she'd made the right decision in choosing Scooby. While it was true that the Appaloosa had been pretty strongly forward when they'd first crossed the fields toward the woods, and he had tested her once or twice early on, he had settled well once Callie reminded him that she was in charge.

And that's exactly the kind of horse I want, she thought as she looped the reins over Scooby's head and led him down a slight hill to let him drink from the cool, clean water of the creek. *I definitely don't want some total packer that's going to let me fall asleep on the trail. Scooby may not be quite as flashy or excitable as some of the endurance champs I've ridden in the past, but underneath that calm exterior he's my kind of horse.*

She waited patiently while Scooby slaked his thirst, staring at the pebbly stream bottom as she planned their future, beginning with a couple of races they might possibly be ready to enter by that spring. The possibilities seemed endless.

When Scooby lifted his head, his muzzle dripping, she led him back up onto the trail. "Ready to move on, bub?" she asked, giving him a solid pat on the neck.

Scooby's only reply was to turn and slobber cold water down her arm. She decided to take that as a yes.

A few minutes later she was mounted and trotting down a slight incline on the trail. Scooby's ears were up and alert, and he seemed to be enjoying the exercise. Callie kept a close eye on the trail ahead, not wanting to miss the turnoff she wanted. She planned to follow the map she'd left in the office, which indicated a path along a tiny tributary of

Willow Creek that led straight into the heart of the huge tract of state forest land that lay between Pine Hollow and the town of Cross County, some ten miles away. She didn't want to overextend Scooby on their first day on the trails, but she wanted to ride far enough to get a better idea about what they needed to do. She also wanted to get away from the usual Pine Hollow student trails, which Max and his staff kept carefully groomed. That was fine for most riders, but Callie wanted to test Scooby's comfort level on different footings, from rocky to muddy to slippery, and she was sure she could find all the variety she needed on the more remote and wilder state forest trails.

"Maybe in a couple of months when the weather improves, we can enter a local twenty-five-miler," she told the horse. "Then we can work our way up from there."

She recognized the right trail when she spotted the tributary, which was hardly more than a trickle at that time of year. Turning her horse, Callie smiled. Now they could really get to work.

They were trotting along the smooth trail a few minutes later when Callie realized that she needed a drink of water almost as much as Scooby had a few minutes earlier. Bringing Scooby down to a walk, she steadied the horse, then took both reins in one hand and twisted around in the saddle. She'd stashed some drinking water with her other supplies in her cantle bag, and it took her only a moment to undo the zipper and dig out the canteen.

She almost lost her balance when Scooby came to an abrupt halt. Leaving the zipper half open, she quickly righted herself and turned to face front again. "Oops," she said, automatically squeezing her legs to get the gelding moving again and then reaching to pat him on the neck. "Okay, boy? What's the problem?"

Scooby snorted, his ears pricked forward and his head high. He hardly seemed to notice Callie's pat.

Callie scanned the forest ahead, wondering what had made the horse stop. Then she shrugged, figuring he had probably heard a deer or something. Or maybe it had happened because she herself had been distracted—maybe her twisting and turning had sent Scooby a confusing signal and that was why he'd reacted that way. Taking both reins in one hand again, she tipped her canteen up and took a long drink, this time making sure she also maintained clear communication with her seat and legs.

Twenty minutes later, they emerged from the heavily wooded trail into a clearing of sorts. The only trees were a few shrubby evergreens, which were clinging to a steep, rocky embankment leading down to a wide spot in the creek.

"Aha," Callie said to her horse. "Here we go." The

clearing was exactly the sort of challenge she'd been looking for. If she and Scooby were to compete at the highest levels of endurance, they would have to take such tricky footing in stride.

Callie didn't rush her horse as they descended, allowing him to pick his way down the slope. Except for a little bit of slipping and sliding near the bottom, the trip was uneventful.

"Good boy!" Callie exclaimed as they reached the edge of the stream. She leaned forward to give him a pat before dismounting. "I'd say that deserves another drink."

Scooby lowered his head and snuffled at the water, taking a few sips and then turning to examine a patch of weeds at the edge of the small stream. He stretched his neck toward the weeds.

"Forget it, buster." Callie pulled his head away and led him back to the flattest part of the clearing. She wedged her foot in the stirrup and started to mount. Just as her right foot left the ground, Scooby suddenly shifted his weight, taking a large step forward and to the right. His ears were pricked again, this time toward the top of the slope they'd just come down.

"Hey!" Callie said, taken by surprise. "Hold still or I'll break my . . ." Her voice trailed off as she saw the horse shift his weight again, lifting his right foreleg off the ground slightly. "Oh no," she muttered, all sorts of horrible scenarios flashing through her mind. They were miles from civilization. What if Scooby had injured himself during that sidestep? He might have stressed or twisted something in his leg. Or, for all she knew, Judy Barker might have missed something on that vet check, thorough as she had been. Scooby could have serious soundness problems that hadn't manifested themselves until that moment. . . .

Forcing herself to remain calm until she knew what was wrong, Callie stepped around to his right side and bent down, squeezing his leg gently until he obediently lifted his foot. Then she leaned over it and immediately saw a large, jagged pebble wedged against the edge of his shoe.

She let out her relief in a whoosh of breath. He had picked up a stone with that awkward sidestep. That was all that was wrong.

"Okay, hold tight a sec, bub," she said soothingly, letting the foot drop. As usual, she had packed a hoof pick in her kit. All she had to do was get it out of the cantle bag and dig out the offending pebble and they could be on their way.

What's with me today, anyway? she wondered as she sifted through the cantle bag. *It's not like me to panic that way before I have any idea what's wrong.* Locating the hoof pick, she patted Scooby on the rump and walked back to his front. *I must be even jumpier than I thought about this whole new-horse thing.*

"Here we are," she said briskly, lifting the horse's leg again with her left hand, hoof pick at the ready in her right. "I'll have that out of there in just a—" Her hand froze in midair as she heard a shout from somewhere nearby.

"Callie!" George Wheeler's voice called cheerfully. "Hey, Callie, it's me!"

Dropping Scooby's foot, Callie slowly straightened and looked over her horse's back. George was riding down the hill toward them.

TWELVE

Callie's head spun, and for a moment she seriously wondered if she was stuck in some kind of bad dream. But the cold metal of the hoof pick in her hand and Scooby's warm presence beside her were very real, and that meant George had to be real, too.

"George," she said carefully as he dismounted and hurried toward her, leaving his mare ground-tied. "What are you doing out here?"

George shrugged, averting his eyes. He nodded toward the hoof pick in her hand. "Looks like you ran into some trouble," he said.

Callie frowned, wondering why he hadn't answered her question. "No big deal," she responded, trying to keep her tone casual. For some reason she really, really didn't want George to know how much his sudden appearance had spooked her. "Scooby picked up a stone, that's all."

"Are you sure?" George looked concerned. "I

guess it's lucky I happened along, then. It's a long, long way back to Pine Hollow, and you wouldn't want to be stranded."

Callie felt her fists clench at her sides. "I'm not stranded," she said as calmly as she could. "Scooby just picked up a pebble, that's all. No biggie."

"Okay, if you say so." George's face expressed his doubt. "I just hope the stone hasn't bruised his foot or anything."

If she hadn't been so angry and freaked out, Callie might have laughed. Who did George think he was dealing with, anyway? It wasn't as if Callie had just started riding yesterday. She'd probably ridden more miles on challenging trails in the past three years than George had seen his whole life. She couldn't even remember how many times she'd popped a pebble or a stubborn clod of dirt out of a horse's hoof during a ride. So where did George get off acting like he'd just galloped to her rescue?

But she forced herself to smile politely. "I'm sure he's fine," she said.

"I don't know." George shook his head and gazed worriedly at Scooby. "You can't be too careful, you know. Joy bruised her foot on a stone just last summer. Why don't you let me take a look, just to be on the safe side?" George held out one pudgy hand, obviously expecting her to hand over the hoof pick.

Callie loosened her grip on the hoof pick,

realizing she'd been squeezing it so hard that it was digging into her hand. She handed it over, wondering why she should feel so unwilling to do so. There was no reason in the world she couldn't dislodge the stone herself. Scooby was her horse. But maybe if she allowed George to satisfy his own ridiculous worry, he would realize that she and Scooby were fine and go away.

"Be my guest," she said as George took the hoof pick and stepped toward Scooby, who was still standing calmly a few yards from the bank of the creek.

Running his hand down Scooby's foreleg, George grabbed the Appaloosa's foot, pulling it up farther than Callie had ever done. Scooby clearly didn't like that. His ears went back and he turned his head to glare at George, his tail swishing. But George seemed oblivious to the horse's discomfort.

"Hold on there, big guy," he said firmly, holding on even more tightly as Scooby jerked his leg a few times.

"Careful," Callie said, taking a step forward. "I don't think he—"

"It's okay," George broke in. "I can handle this."

Callie wasn't convinced of that. But before she could figure out a tactful way to say so, Scooby took the situation into his own hooves. With one strong yank, he pulled his foot out of George's grip and skittered to the side, snorting. Nearby, George's horse, Joyride, raised her head from the grassy patch she'd found and let out a slightly nervous snort of her own.

Good, Callie thought, moving forward quickly and taking hold of Scooby's head before he could decide to take off. *Maybe now George will give up on the Dudley Do-Right bit and let me handle this.*

George glanced quickly at Joyride, then returned his attention to Scooby. "Whew! See what I mean?" He shook his head and patted the Appaloosa on the shoulder. "He's pretty jumpy. That stone must be lodged in there pretty good. It's probably so painful that he's afraid to have me touch it."

Callie grimaced. With the way George was man-handling Scooby's foot, it was no wonder the gelding was jumpy. Why did George have to show up and make things more difficult, anyway?

She stopped to think about that. It was pretty strange that George was there at all. She was sure she would have noticed if he'd followed her all the way from Pine Hollow, and there really wasn't much chance of them running into each other randomly—not in this remote part of the forest. She glanced up at the trail at the top of the rocky slope, wondering if George was some kind of secret mountain man, tracking her by following broken twigs and hoofprints in the mud.

Then she shook her head, feeling slightly foolish. It was stupid to freak herself out that way. Encountering George out there was a coincidence, that was all. A horrible, ridiculous, unfortunate coincidence. She cleared her throat and glanced at George, who was moving toward Scooby with the hoof pick again. "By the way," she said as casually as she could manage, "what made you decide to ride out this way? It's kind of off the beaten path."

George didn't answer. "I'd better give it another try," he said. "Come on, Scooby. Let's take care of that foot of yours, okay?"

Callie watched as he patted her horse for a moment, then bent to lift Scooby's foot again. Propping the foot against his leg, he set to work with the hoof pick.

"Wow, this is really wedged in here," George commented after a moment. "It's going to take some elbow grease to pry it out. Lucky thing I happened to see that map in the office. Otherwise you would have had to—"

Callie didn't hear the rest of what he said. "The map?" she interrupted. "What map?"

But she already knew the answer, even before George straightened up slightly to respond. "Your map," he said with a shrug. "The one you drew to show where you were going today. When I saw how far out you were riding, I figured I'd come on out here and make sure everything was okay. You know, new horse and all."

"*What?*" Callie couldn't contain her fury anymore. "You've got to be kidding! Why would you do that?"

George looked startled. "Well, I just thought— Um, whatever. Besides, you haven't lived here that long. And it's not like you've spent a whole lot of time on these trails, so I—"

"So you decided to appoint yourself my personal baby-sitter?" Callie could hardly believe this was happening. It was too much—like something out of a nightmare. Suddenly another question occurred to her. "And how did you see that map, anyway? Maureen or Red should've put it in the daybook so that it wouldn't get lost."

Instead of responding to that, George bent over Scooby's hoof again. The gelding shifted uneasily, but George kept a firm grip on the hoof and after a moment the horse stood still. "Good boy," George murmured. "Just let me help you out here, okay?"

Callie realized she had taken a few steps back, away from George. To her own surprise, she felt fear—real, palm-sweating, gut-twisting fear— welling up alongside her anger, confusion, and disgust. She and George were out in the woods, miles from anywhere, all alone. For the first time, as she watched him bend over her horse's hoof, George didn't seem like the same irritating, bumbling loser she had known for months. Suddenly he had become someone mysterious, unpredictable, and sort of scary.

Get a grip, girl, Callie thought sharply, irritated by her own wild thoughts. *This is still George Wheeler we're talking about. George the nerd, the annoying but harmless one, the junior-class wimp. He may be clueless and weird, but that doesn't make him an ax murderer or something.*

She was taking a few deep breaths, trying to calm herself, when out of the corner of her eye she saw George make a quick, sharp movement with the hoof pick. She blinked and focused on what he was doing. Scooby's ears were flattened again, and this time the gelding wasn't giving up. He jerked his leg sharply, causing George to lose his grip.

"What was that?" Callie asked, a little anxious. She wouldn't have let George get near Scooby's feet if she hadn't thought he knew what he was doing. But he was definitely acting weird. "Did you get it out?"

Instead of replying immediately, George straightened up and gestured to her with the hoof pick. "Come here, check this out."

Callie slowly stepped forward, strangely reluctant to approach him but forcing herself to act as if nothing were wrong. "What is it?"

George wrestled Scooby's foot up, though he only

managed it by leaning hard on the gelding's shoulder. "See? This shoe is totally loose. It's a good thing we caught this before it got any worse or you could have had real problems."

Callie stared, her mind refusing to accept what she was seeing. Scooby's metal shoe was partially off, one nail twisted out slightly at an awkward angle. But that just couldn't be. The blacksmith had just shod Scooby on Saturday, after he'd come to Pine Hollow. All four shoes had been tight and properly fitted then, and they had been just as tight that morning when they'd set off. Callie would bet her life on that.

Then how did it come loose now? she wondered, cold fingers of fear tickling her spine. *Did it happen somehow at the same time he picked up that stone?*

But she knew that wasn't it. She'd lifted the horse's foot herself after that had happened. There was no way she could have missed noticing such a major problem with the shoe. No way at all.

"It looks pretty bad," George said, waving the hoof pick to punctuate the comment.

That was when Callie noticed that the tip of the metal hoof pick was bent at an odd angle. And she finally had to face the truth. George had done it. He had intentionally loosened her horse's shoe, making him virtually unridable.

But why? she wondered desperately, hiding her face from George by bending closer over Scooby's hoof. *What in the world would make him do something like that?*

She shook her head, pushing the question out of her mind. She would have to figure that out later.

Because at the moment, she had a much more important question to deal with. What was she supposed to do now?

Stevie shivered slightly as a cold breeze lifted the hair off her forehead. She was perched on the rustic wooden hitching fence outside Cross County Stables, waiting for Phil. "Brr," she commented to no one in particular. "It's starting to feel like Christmas now." She shivered again, though not from the weather. The Starlight Ride was the following evening—Christmas Eve. Stevie was a little surprised at how much she was looking forward to it.

She jammed her hard hat on her head, hoping it would help keep her warm until she started riding. A moment later she finally spotted Phil riding toward her across the fields from the direction of his house. She stood and waited for him.

"Hi!" Phil called when he got close enough, bringing Teddy down from a trot to a walk. "Sorry I'm late. My little sister needed help with her pony.

She's practicing over cross rails today in our pasture, and my parents are practically hysterical about making sure her girth is good and tight."

Stevie stood back until Phil dismounted, then stepped forward to kiss him hello. "That's okay," she said. "I just got here a few minutes ago. So, is A.J. going to be joining us or what?"

"I don't know. I tried to reach him all day yesterday, but no luck." Phil looped his reins over Teddy's neck and led him forward beside Stevie as they headed slowly toward the stable. "I finally just left a message with his dad, telling him we'd be here today. I don't know if he'll show or not."

"Oh." Stevie was disappointed. "I was hoping maybe he'd have some news."

Phil shrugged. "Me too. Come on, let's go find you something to ride."

The two of them were tacking up a horse for Stevie a few minutes later when they heard a familiar voice calling their names. "It's A.J.!" Stevie exclaimed. "He made it!" She raised her voice slightly. "We're in here, A.J."

A.J.'s freckled face appeared over the stall door. "Hey," he greeted them. "What's up?"

"Hi!" Phil said. "Where've you been, buddy? I tried calling you all weekend."

"Did you hear from that woman?" Stevie asked at

the same time, almost dropping the bridle she was holding in her excitement. "Is she your mother?"

A.J. frowned. "What is this, the Spanish Inquisition?" he muttered.

Stevie noticed for the first time that he looked kind of grumpy. *Uh-oh,* she thought. *Maybe she still hasn't called and it's getting him down.*

Before she could ask again, A.J. sighed heavily. "Okay, I know you two aren't going to leave me alone until I tell you," he said. "So yes, that woman called yesterday. And no, she's not my birth mother."

Stevie's jaw dropped. "She's not?" she blurted out. "But I was so sure—"

"Sorry, A.J.," Phil said, tentatively reaching out to pat A.J. on the arm.

A.J. jerked his arm back. "Whatever," he said sharply. "Now come on, are we going to ride or what?"

"But, A.J., what did she say?" Stevie asked uncertainly, not willing to let the topic drop just yet. "Are you sure she's no relation? Maybe she's, like, some kind of biological aunt or cousin or something." Seeing A.J.'s expression darken, she changed directions hastily. "Anyway, even if that lead was a bust, it doesn't mean the next one won't turn out to be the real deal."

A.J. rolled his eyes. "Give it up, Stevie. That woman isn't my relative any more than you are. And you know what? I'm glad. I'm starting to think this whole deal—looking for my birth parents, I mean—is a big fat mistake."

"What?" Phil sounded startled. "But I thought you were into this."

Stevie nodded. "You'll feel better if you know where you came from," she said encouragingly. "What your roots are and stuff, you know?"

"I'm not so sure about that." A.J.'s scowl deepened. "Why should I care about finding someone who doesn't care about me? I mean, she gave me up, right? She didn't want me or she would've kept me." He shrugged. "I think maybe I'm better off just letting the whole thing drop."

Stevie couldn't believe her ears. How could A.J. feel that way? *If it were me, I wouldn't rest until I tracked down my birth mother*, she thought. *I would have to know the truth.*

She didn't think saying so would help A.J., though. He was obviously in a pessimistic place after the setback with the woman in the photo, and Stevie couldn't help feeling responsible for that. After all, she was the one who'd found the picture in the first place.

She decided to do the only thing she could think of to make it up to A.J., at least for the moment—

change the subject. "Okay then," she said briskly, ignoring Phil's surprised glance. "Why don't you go tack up, A.J.? I think we could all use a nice, relaxing ride right about now."

At that same moment, Callie was feeling anything but relaxed. "What's wrong with you?" she asked George. "You must have loosened it with the hoof pick." She stopped just short of accusing him of doing it intentionally, a little fearful of how he might react to that. A week ago she had thought him totally predictable. Now she wasn't so sure.

George wasn't looking at her. He was gazing into the clear, cold water tumbling into the still pool beside them. "Why would I do something like that?"

Callie took a deep breath. To her own surprise, she was feeling dangerously close to bursting into tears. Why would George come all the way out here into the wilderness after her just to sabotage her horse's shoe? It was crazy. And worse than that, she wasn't sure how to deal with it. She was prepared for a lot of emergencies on the trail, from cuts and scratches to bee stings to dehydration. But this was a totally different situation. Even though Scooby had gone shoeless until a couple of days earlier, she definitely didn't want to risk his soundness on the rough footing of the state parklands. And she hadn't bought Easy Boots in his size yet, so she didn't have any with her to use, even if she could manage to pull the shoe off the rest of the way.

But this is nuts, she thought, gathering her wits after a moment of near panic. *Of course I'm prepared for this kind of thing, too. George or no George, it's totally possible that my horse could somehow lose or loosen a shoe during a race or a training session. What would I normally do?*

The answer came to her immediately. She would lead Scooby to the nearest road, which probably wasn't more than a half mile away to the east, then use her cell phone to call Pine Hollow for Red or someone to come and pick them up with one of the stable's trailers. It seemed so simple all of a sudden that she felt like laughing out loud.

Controlling that impulse, she patted Scooby comfortingly and then reached into the cantle bag for the phone. "Excuse me," she told George icily. "I've got to call for a ride."

"What do you mean?" George blinked in surprise as Callie pressed the power button and the phone came to life with a bleep. "What's that?"

"It's a phone. Perhaps you've heard of them," Callie said, not bothering to keep the sarcasm from her voice. Better to have George think she was angry with him—which she was—than to let him see that she was also scared.

"Oh!" George stepped toward her. "Here, let me do that. I'll call Pine Hollow while you hold on to Scooby."

"That's okay," Callie protested. "I can do—"

She gasped as George grabbed for the phone, moving faster than she'd thought he could. "No, no, I insist!" he exclaimed, pulling the phone out of her grip. "I'll just call the stable, and then I'll help you—oops!"

Callie gasped again, watching as the cell phone slid out of George's grip. The whole scene seemed to slip into slow motion as the phone flew up in a wide arc before falling toward the streambed. Snapping out of her trancelike state, she lunged for it, trying to catch it before it hit the ground. But she was too late. The phone smashed against the rocky slope, a large piece of the black plastic casing snapping off and whizzing to the ground. The rest of the phone bounced, landing a split second later with a splash in the stream, which swept it away.

"Ohmigosh! I'm sorry!" George's gray eyes were wide. "It slipped, Callie, I swear! I'm really sorry. I'll buy you a new one, I promise."

Callie's heart was pounding at triple its usual speed. *Now what?* she thought desperately, staring at the cracked piece of black plastic lying at the edge of the stream. *Now how do I get out of this?*

Because suddenly she was completely certain that George wasn't sorry. He'd done it on purpose—all of it. First he'd followed her into the woods, far from civilization. Then he'd found a way to put her horse out of commission. And now he'd effectively removed her last link with anyone who could help her.

"Don't worry, though," George said, interrupting her thoughts. He gestured toward his horse, who was still grazing nearby. "We can both ride Joy back to the stable—we'll stay at a walk and lead Scooby so that he doesn't hurt himself."

He took a step toward Callie, smiling eagerly. Callie stepped backward until her back was pressed against Scooby's warm, solid flank. The edge of the saddle cut into her shoulder, but she hardly noticed.

It's crazy, she thought, feeling panic well up and constrict her throat until she could hardly breathe. *Anyone who would do all that stuff on purpose would have to be crazy.*

But she just couldn't shake her conviction that George had done just that—which meant that he *was* crazy. Totally off his rocker.

And that was the scariest thought of all.

THIRTEEN

Okay, so now what? Callie thought as George took another step toward her. *How do I get myself out of this one?*

For a moment she was tempted to turn and pull herself into Scooby's saddle. She could be a good quarter of a mile away by the time George could clamber up the slope to his horse and follow her. And while Joyride, with her long Trakehner legs, could easily outrun Scooby on the flat, the sturdy, compact Appaloosa would have an advantage in the rougher territory of the thick woods beyond the clearing they were in.

Get a grip, she told herself firmly, banishing the idea immediately. She couldn't risk Scooby's soundness, and perhaps his life, just because she was having a paranoia attack.

Still, as she glanced at George again, she knew there was no way she could go along with George's plan. He was still advancing toward her, a weird little smile on his round face.

"Come on," he said, stretching his hand toward her. "Give me Scooby's lead. I'll help you bring him up the hill."

"I don't think so," Callie said, easing past Scooby's head with the intention of putting the horse between her and George. She had no idea what she would do then, but she hoped the slight distance would allow her to take a few deep breaths, control her panic, and get her mind working again.

"Huh?" George blinked in surprise as Callie shoved Scooby's head up so that she could duck underneath. She guessed that her nervousness was rubbing off on the gelding, since his ears were pinned back and he was shifting uneasily, his hindquarters rotating slightly toward George. "Come on, Callie. I just want to help. Give me the—"

Scooby clearly decided he'd had enough. Letting out a loud snort, he whirled around, almost knocking Callie over as he kicked out swiftly and strongly with one hind leg.

George was staring so intently at Callie that he didn't see the kick coming. He yelped in surprise and pain as Scooby's hoof connected firmly with his upper thigh. Stumbling backward, he grabbed at his leg and tripped over a rock. As Callie grabbed

Scooby's reins, she saw George fall. She winced as his head connected solidly with a tree stump; there was a sickening crack.

"George!" she gasped, her fear dissipating as George slumped to the rocky ground, one hand flopping into the cold water of the stream. Her heart in her throat, Callie quickly murmured a few soothing words to Scooby, who already seemed to be calming down. Leading him forward and leaving him ground-tied at a safe distance, she cautiously approached George.

She leaned toward him, gripped by the sudden certainty that his eyes were going to fly open and he was going to grab at her throat.

Stop it! she told herself fiercely. *This isn't some cheesy horror movie. This is real life. George is really hurt, and I'm the only one who can help him.*

That helped her focus. Kneeling down beside him, hardly feeling the sharp stones cutting into her knees through the thin fabric of her breeches, she tried to remember what she'd learned in the first-aid course she'd taken a couple of years earlier.

"George?" she croaked, touching him tentatively on the shoulder. She swallowed hard and tried again, more loudly this time. "George? Are you okay?"

There was no response. George was out cold.

Callie glanced at his chest and was relieved to see it rising and falling steadily. He seemed to be breathing normally, and she couldn't see any blood where his head had struck the stump.

I probably shouldn't try to move him, though, she thought with an odd little shiver of relief, remembering a lecture on the dangers of neck and spine injuries. *He's probably got a concussion at the very least, which means he needs professional help. I shouldn't even touch him. I should just go call the paramedics or something.*

She bit her lip, wondering if she was being completely honest with herself. What would she do if this were Stevie lying unconscious in the cold December woods? Or Scott? Or almost anyone else, even a total stranger?

I would probably try to revive them, she thought, glancing toward the cold water running past. *Then if we were pretty sure there were no broken bones or anything, I'd try to get them into the saddle and lead them out to the road so that we could flag down a car and get help as soon as possible.*

She shuddered as she imagined doing all that with George. Waking him up, seeing those round, grayish eyes fixed on her again. Touching him, feeling for injuries. Letting him lean on her as she helped him toward Joyride . . .

No way, she thought, feeling like the world's

biggest coward as she stood and backed away from George's still, pudgy form. *I can't do it.*

She stared at him, trying to convince herself that she was being irrational. And she definitely was; she knew it. Looking at George now, how could she ever have been frightened of him?

Nonetheless, she knew there was no way in the world that she could completely forget the panic and powerlessness she'd felt just moments earlier. There was also no way she could really believe that this had all been some kind of huge coincidence, a run of plain old bad luck with no sinister intentions on George's part. No, he had been up to no good—Callie was as certain of that as she was of her own name. She hated feeling helpless, especially in her own element, and George had made her feel that way. She wasn't going to forget that anytime soon.

"Stay here," she said aloud, even though she knew that George couldn't hear her. "I'll go get help."

Forcing herself to crouch beside him again, she quickly felt for his pulse and put a hand near his face to check that his breath really was coming in and out as it should. Noticing that his fingers were still trailing in the stream, she yanked at his sleeve until his arm was resting by his side. Then she backed away and glanced at the two horses, which were both grazing contentedly by that time.

Moving quickly—was it because she wanted to get help as soon as possible or because she was afraid George might wake up before she got away?—Callie loosened Scooby's girth until she could yank the pad from beneath the saddle.

"Sorry, boy," she murmured. "I need to borrow this."

She took the saddle pad and draped it over George's body, hoping the fleece would keep him from getting too chilled. It would be the better part of an hour before help could possibly reach him, and despite the bright midday sunshine, the air was chilly. Trying not to think about that, Callie returned to Scooby, clipping a lead line onto him. Moments later she was in Joyride's saddle, with Scooby trailing along at the mare's flank.

"Okay, guys," she told the horses, already feeling a little better now that she was in the saddle again, with a real plan of action. Trying not to glance at George, who looked pathetic and pale against the stony stream bank, she patted Joyride on the withers and checked to make sure that Scooby was following quietly. "Ready to get out of here? Because I know I am."

Without another backward look, Callie urged Joyride into a brisk walk and turned to the east, heading toward the road.

———

Lisa stared at the box in the middle of her bedroom floor, wondering what she was waiting for.

I should just return it already, she thought, a little annoyed with herself. *That's what I decided to do. So what's the problem?*

But the thought of doing it—of taking the gift she'd chosen for Alex and returning it to the store—made her feel a little queasy. Wouldn't returning the gift mean turning her back on the possibility that they might get back together? Wouldn't it mean giving up on something that had been so wonderful—something that could be wonderful again if they just gave it a chance?

Maybe I should wait, she thought uncertainly, her mind flashing past image after image of herself and Alex together—their first kiss, the two of them dancing together at her prom the previous spring, their reunion after her return from California that summer, and on and on. So many good times. *It feels really wrong to just assume it's all over between us.*

She stared at the box again. It would be easy enough to shove it into the closet again, leave it there until things were settled. It wasn't as though she couldn't come up with the money to buy Red and Denise a wedding gift otherwise. All she had to do was dip into the Christmas money that her relatives had already sent.

The phone rang, and Lisa jumped to her feet, a

little relieved at the interruption. *I just hope it's not Aunt Marianne again,* she thought with a grimace as she hurried into the hall. *If she tells me one more time how absolutely wonderful the schools are in New Jersey or starts babbling again about all the shopping I can do at the amazing outlet mall near her house, I'll scream.*

"Hello?" she said cautiously as she picked up the phone. "Atwood residence, Lisa speaking."

"Hi, it's Scott."

Lisa gulped. Christmas Eve was the next day. He had to be calling about the Starlight Ride. She still hadn't really given him an answer, and she knew she couldn't put it off any longer. "Oh. Hi."

"How's it going?" Scott asked. "I was just wondering if you've made up your mind. If you're going to do me the honor of being my date tomorrow night."

Lisa hesitated, wondering what to say. She didn't know any other guy her age who would put it just that way—*do me the honor.* It reminded her of how different Scott was, how interesting and fun it had been getting to know him better. Not to mention that intense, mind-bending kiss . . .

But then there was Alex. Hadn't she just been thinking that she wasn't ready to give up on their relationship? If she went on the Starlight Ride with Scott, it would be their third date. That was starting to go beyond "seeing other people" and into the realm of getting involved. Was Lisa ready to make that choice?

I wish I'd thought to ask Stevie and Carole for their advice about this, she thought. *Maybe they could help me figure out what I want.*

Thinking of her best friends brought back to mind the ever-present and ever-horrible idea that she might be totally on her own soon if her mother had her way. Before long the only advice Lisa would be able to get from Carole and Stevie would be via long-distance phone calls or e-mail. The thought sent a pang through her, painful and raw.

"Lisa?" Scott's voice said in her ear. "Are you still there?"

"I'm here." Lisa cleared her throat. "And the answer is yes. I'd love to go on the Starlight Ride with you."

"Great!" Scott sounded pleased and a little surprised.

He went on to say something about picking her up the next evening, though Lisa hardly heard him. She was too busy trying to hold back the tears that threatened to overflow as she thought about leaving her friends—and everything else that meant home to her—far behind. No matter what it meant regarding her relationship with Scott and/or Alex, she was glad that she would be going on the Starlight Ride the next night. It would give her a chance to be with her friends, and there might not be many of those chances left.

It will be sort of like old times, she thought with a sudden stab of nostalgia. *Like our first Starlight Ride together, the year it actually snowed. Maybe for one night I can pretend we're all still thirteen years old and none of us has to worry yet about stuff like college and boyfriends and moving.*

As she said good-bye to Scott and hung up, Lisa took a few deep breaths, trying to bring her emotions back under control. As she wandered back into her room, her gaze locked once again on the box in the middle of the floor. Alex's present. For a second she felt guilty about her decision to go on the Starlight Ride. Was she using Scott? Was she betraying Alex?

No, she decided, grabbing the box and walking toward the closet. Opening the door, she stood on tiptoes until she could shove the box onto the highest shelf. *Alex and I agreed to date other people. And I already talked to Scott about how complicated things are between me and Alex. He's mature enough to deal with that, however it turns out. Only time will tell. And why sit home alone in the meantime?*

Callie peered out over the half door of Scooby's stall as she heard voices approaching from the direction of the stable entryway. It had been an hour and a half since she had ridden away from George's still form out there in the woods, and even now that they were all back at the stable, safe and sound, she still couldn't quite believe everything that had happened. At the moment George was walking between a man and a woman—the paramedics who had brought him back to Pine Hollow. The three of them were chatting easily, though Callie couldn't hear the exact words.

She ducked down out of sight as the trio passed and then stopped just down the aisle in front of Joyride's stall. She was relieved that George seemed to be okay, but that didn't mean she was ready to face him. She could still feel the ghost of the panic that had gripped her out there when she had seen the oddly twisted metal of that hoof pick, and then as she had watched her cell phone fly into the stream. Now that she was back in the safe, familiar surroundings of Pine Hollow, it all seemed kind of foolish. But that didn't mean she was going to be able to forget it anytime soon.

It was just a big misunderstanding, that's all, she told herself for the umpteenth time, leaning against the back of the door and watching as Scooby selected a mouthful of hay. *Another example of George's general social cluelessness. And his clumsiness.*

But as many times as she told herself that, she couldn't quite banish from her imagination the image of George twisting the hoof pick to wrench up the edge of Scooby's shoe. Callie couldn't make herself believe, even now, that that had been simple clumsiness.

She waited until the voices moved away again. When she was sure that George was well out of sight, she gave Scooby a pat and slipped out of the stall. Heading for the back exit at the far end of the aisle, she broke into a jog. Soon she was walking swiftly across the fields toward home, trying to shake the irrational feeling that she was being followed. Frequent glances over her shoulder proved that there was no one there, but it didn't stop her heart from pounding.

Even an hour later, safely locked behind her own bedroom door with the windows latched and the curtains drawn, Callie couldn't quite seem to stop shaking.

FOURTEEN

"Stevie!" May Grover called urgently. "I need a hoof pick, and there aren't any in the tack room!"

Stevie reached around and pulled a hoof pick out of the back pocket of her jeans. "Here's one," she said, handing it to the younger girl. "You can put it back in the tack room when you're finished with it."

"Thanks!" May raced off toward her horse's stall.

Stevie glanced around, expecting to see one or more of May's classmates approaching with more questions or problems. She had been helping the Starlight Riders with last-minute preparations for the past half hour with hardly a pause for breath. But at the moment the only person she saw coming toward her was Phil.

"Hi," he said with the special, private smile he saved just for her. "How's it going?"

Stevie hurried toward him and reached out for a hug. "These kids are running me ragged!" she exclaimed dramatically. "I think I'm too tired for the actual Starlight Ride!"

"Don't even think it," Phil warned jokingly, squeezing her tight. "I've been looking forward to this for weeks." He leaned down, his lips almost brushing her forehead. "Remember the first time we went on the Starlight Ride together?"

"Hey! Get a room," Scott's voice broke in before Stevie could answer. "This is a stable, not Lovers' Lane."

Stevie grinned and pulled away from Phil, glancing over her shoulder at Scott. "Says who?"

Phil raised a hand in greeting to Scott. "So where's your date?" he asked.

"She's tacking up my horse." Scott grinned sheepishly. "You guys know I'm not too good with that stuff. I can never remember which way the saddle pad goes on or which buckles you're supposed to use with the girth."

"Yeah, right," Stevie teased him. "You're just looking for a way to get someone else to do your work for you."

"Hey, I offered to help." Scott held up both hands in protest. "But for some reason, Lisa seemed to think she could do the job faster without my assistance."

Phil laughed. "Good deal. Now all you have to do is sit back and wait for the fun part."

"It *is* going to be fun, isn't it?" Stevie commented happily. She couldn't wait for the ride to start. She also couldn't wait for it to be over so that she could give Phil his gift. The box from The Saddlery was carefully wrapped and hidden in a plastic bag in her cubbyhole. Forcing her mind away from that topic—she didn't want to get overexcited and give away her secret too soon—she glanced again at Scott. "I wish Callie were here, though," she commented. "You never really told us why she decided not to come."

Scott shrugged. "She never really told me," he said. "She just said something about being tired after training Scooby so hard."

"Really?" Stevie frowned slightly. "But that doesn't sound right. I mean, I know she was out on the trails for hours yesterday, but I didn't think she even came to the stable today. I remember hearing Denise saying something about turning Scooby out in the back paddock for a while to get some exercise."

"I know. Callie hung out at home today. Doing the whole Christmas Eve thing, I guess." Scott shrugged again. "But I guess she and Scooby were out for a long time yesterday, like you said. And then with George's accident . . ."

Stevie nodded, wondering briefly what that was all about. All she knew was that George had ended up deep in the woods somehow, been kicked by a horse, and ended up being rescued by Callie and the paramedics. She'd only gathered that much from the younger riders, who had been buzzing about it all day when they weren't talking about the Starlight Ride. *I'll have to get the whole story after this is over,* she thought, squashing her curiosity for the moment. *That's yet another reason it's too bad Callie didn't come tonight. She could've filled us in on what really happened.*

Still, she supposed it really wasn't too surprising that Callie had decided not to come along. The temperature had dropped overnight, and for anyone who didn't know how wonderful the Starlight Ride was, the weather could make the evening ride seem a little daunting. A couple of the younger students who had signed up to ride had called earlier that day to cancel, and Stevie suspected that Scott wouldn't be there either if he didn't have a date with Lisa.

Thinking about that distracted Stevie from her other thoughts. By her count, this would be the third time Lisa and Scott had been out together. One date was weird enough, but three was way beyond that. What if Scott and Lisa got serious about each other? What if they became a real couple? It would change everything in their little group.

"Stevie!" Sarah Anne Porter's shrill voice snapped

her back to reality. "I can't get Barq to let me put the bit in his mouth!"

Stevie sighed. "I'll come help you," she assured the younger girl. "Barq can be stubborn about that sometimes." Shooting Phil and Scott an apologetic glance, she hurried off to the rescue.

A few minutes later Barq was safely tacked up and Stevie was hurrying toward the rest room to wash the horse slobber off her hands. If she moved fast, she would have just enough time to tack up Belle and then help Max with the preride inspection.

And then the fun begins, she thought eagerly. *I'll find a nice, private spot to ride near the end of the line, and then Phil and I can—*

Her thoughts broke off as she opened the door to the women's rest room and caught a whiff of rancid smoke. "Ugh," she said, waving a hand in front of her face. "Is someone smoking in here?"

The answer presented itself almost immediately when she spotted Maureen leaning against the cracked porcelain sink with a lit cigarette in her fingers. "Stevie," the stable hand said casually, waving the cigarette in her general direction. "What's up?"

"Are you crazy?" Stevie put her hands on her hips and stared at the stable hand. "I know you're new around here and all, but I'm sure Max told you he doesn't allow smoking anywhere in the stable. It's, like, one of his strictest rules."

Maureen laughed and raised the cigarette to her lips, inhaling slowly before responding. "Is it really?" she asked, blowing out smoke along with the words. "Max has so many rules around this place that it's hard to keep track of which ones he's serious about."

Stevie frowned, annoyed at Maureen's sarcastic tone. "He's serious about all of them," she snapped. "Otherwise he wouldn't bother."

"Whatever." Maureen waved her hand in Stevie's direction again, making her cough. "Why don't you run along now? You're supposed to be going on this ride tonight with the rest of the kiddies, aren't you?"

Stevie's blood boiled. If there was one thing she hated, it was being dismissed and treated like a child. *Chill*, she warned herself as Maureen stubbed her cigarette out on the sink and left without another word. *It's not worth it. You can deal with it later.*

Making a mental note to do just that, she quickly washed her hands and then hurried out, to find Phil waiting for her. "What's wrong?" he asked immediately.

"Nothing." Stevie took a deep breath, vowing to forget about the annoying encounter with Maureen until after the Starlight Ride—and her gift exchange with Phil.

She smiled immediately, imagining the look on

his face when he saw those beautiful chaps. She couldn't wait.

"Come on," she said, grabbing Phil by the hand. "Let's go get tacked up."

Lisa leaned over from her position in the saddle to shorten her left stirrup, then reached forward to pat Eve on the shoulder. "Almost time to go, sweetie," she murmured to the gray mare.

Eve stood quietly, though her ears flicked back and forth with interest as people and horses hurried by in all directions. It was almost time to set out, and everyone was scrambling to get ready.

Lisa had been helping younger riders with their preparations ever since she and Scott had arrived half an hour earlier. The last she had seen of Scott, he was standing with Congo's lead line in his hand, chatting with a ten-year-old rider named Kenny, who suddenly seemed to have developed a fear of the dark. Or maybe it was a fear of his pony, Nickel—Lisa wasn't quite sure.

I'm sure Scott will make him feel better either way, she thought, running the fingers of one hand over the pommel of her saddle. *He's good at making people feel comfortable, no matter what the situation.*

She smiled slightly as she thought about that. Then she sighed. What was she going to do about

Scott? She had hoped that seeing him that night would help her decide. But all it had done was make her realize that there really was something between them—an attraction, a mutual interest that couldn't be denied. Did that mean she didn't still have feelings for Alex?

No way, she thought. *My heart still feels like it's going to shatter into a million pieces when I think that Alex and I may be broken up for good. I can't imagine what it would be like to go on, live the whole rest of my life without him in it.* She grimaced as she remembered shoving that box into her closet the day before. *I can't even imagine what it would be like to return that stupid sweater I picked out for him.*

She sighed, loosening her grip on Eve's reins as she realized she was clenching them tightly. Yes, it definitely hurt to picture her life without Alex. But did it hurt as much now as it had when they'd first broken up a few weeks earlier? Did it hurt a little less when she was with Scott? She wasn't sure what to think about those questions. She wasn't even sure she wanted to know the answers.

Lisa did her best to push all that out of her mind when she spotted Scott approaching, still leading Congo. "Hey," he greeted her with that easy smile of his, the one that crinkled the edges of his eyes slightly. "There you are."

"Here I am," she said lightly, deciding it was time

to stop brooding and try to enjoy herself. "How's Kenny?"

Scott chuckled. "Still nervous. But I think he'll be okay."

At that moment Lisa heard Max's voice calling for attention outside. Along with everyone else in the wide entryway, as well as the riders who were already gathered outside in the stable yard, she turned to listen.

Max quickly ran through the rules of the ride. No cantering, no passing the leader, no leaving the marked trail, and so on. Lisa listened politely, though she'd heard it all many times before. Glancing over at Scott, she was just in time to see him swing himself into Congo's saddle without the help of a mounting block. He might not have been a regular rider, but he was athletic enough to hold his own when necessary.

"Okay," Lisa said as Max finished his speech and everyone started chattering excitedly. "Here we go! Are you ready?"

"Absolutely." Scott gave her a meaningful smile. "I can't wait."

Lisa blushed slightly and glanced out the door. She watched Rachel Hart ride forward, pausing at the stable entrance just long enough to brush the battered horseshoe hanging there with her fingers. The lucky horseshoe was a long-standing Pine

Hollow tradition—the story went that nobody who touched the horseshoe before a ride had ever been seriously hurt—and Lisa couldn't help smiling as she watched the whole parade of young riders carefully reaching out to touch the well-worn piece of metal. Some barely slowed down long enough to tap it, while others lingered, running their hands over its whole surface. But nobody passed by without remembering to touch it one way or another.

"Ready to go?" Red called from outside as the last few younger students hurried out.

A cheer went up from the gathered riders. Through the doorway, Lisa saw Stevie step forward and hand Rachel the leader's torch. The younger girl shifted both reins to one hand and solemnly accepted the torch, holding it up proudly as she took her place at the head of the line. Each year Max chose the best overall intermediate rider to lead the procession, and that year Rachel had won the honor. She was riding Starlight, Carole's horse, for the occasion, which Lisa thought was very appropriate. It was right after the Starlight Ride some years earlier that Carole had discovered that her father had bought the lively gelding for her as a special Christmas gift.

"We're ready," Rachel said when she and Starlight were in position, her soft voice carrying across the crisp evening air.

Lisa quickly urged Eve forward and touched the

208

lucky horseshoe herself, then joined the others in the stable yard. Rachel and the other riders near the front were already walking their horses toward the gate, heading for the trail through the fields marked out by flickering torches. It wasn't quite dark yet, though the sun had set and a rosy glow lay over the fields and pastures. Lisa knew that many of the younger riders had probably never ridden at night before. She still remembered how it felt to be out there in the woods on horseback for the first time—the familiar trails looked so mysterious, almost magical, in the flickering light of the lanterns along the way, and the sound of hoofbeats seemed muffled by the darkness.

The next hour passed quickly. Lisa found herself relaxing more and more, forgetting her problems at least temporarily as she joined in singing holiday carols and chatted with Scott and her other friends. As the procession made its way toward the woods between the stable and the town of Willow Creek, they passed several brightly lit farmhouses and twinkling Christmas trees. For the first time that year, Lisa felt a little bit of holiday spirit seeping through her. By the time they all entered the torchlit trail through the forest, it was fully dark.

This is nice, she thought as she glanced at Scott riding beside her on the wide trail. *I'm really glad I came.*

When they reached the town square a little later, a small crowd was gathered to greet them near a crackling bonfire. Along with Max and Denise, who had driven over in Pine Hollow's truck with a generous supply of hot chocolate and snacks, Lisa saw many of the younger riders' families, as well as other townspeople who just came to enjoy the festivities. Even the mayor was there, chatting with constituents over a steaming cup of cocoa.

"Wow," Scott commented. "Quite a turnout."

Lisa nodded and smiled. "Didn't I tell you this was a major tradition?"

"You did." Scott laughed and dismounted, then held out a hand to hold Eve steady as Lisa did likewise. He even insisted on helping her loosen Eve's girth, although she was perfectly capable of doing it herself. "Now," he said when both their mounts were comfortable, "if you don't mind staying with the horses, I'll go get us something to drink. Okay?"

"Okay." Lisa took hold of Eve and Congo and watched as Scott threaded his way through the crowd, pausing every few seconds to shake someone's hand or slap them on the back.

Then she turned and squinted in the uncertain light of the bonfire and the surrounding buildings, looking for her friends. A few yards away, she saw Stevie and Phil in the middle of a small group, talking and laughing. Back at the edge of the square,

Carole and Cam were standing close together, apparently lost in a world all their own as they talked quietly with each other.

Looks like they're all having fun, Lisa thought with a pang of sadness. What would it be like to live somewhere far away from her friends? To only talk to them on the phone a couple of times a week, if that?

She turned and saw Scott heading toward her, a Styrofoam cup in each hand and a few napkins tucked under his arm. When he reached her, he carefully handed her one of the cups. "Here you go," he said. "Careful, it's hot."

"Thanks." Lisa accepted the cup gratefully. It felt nice and warm against her hands, even through her winter riding gloves. Blowing on the surface, she let the steam caress her face. "So what do you think of the Starlight Ride so far?"

"It's great," Scott said. "I'm really—"

"Yo, Scott!" A guy Lisa didn't recognize came loping toward them. "How's it going, man?"

Lisa sighed, annoyed at the interruption. But Scott smiled at the other guy. "Hey, Barry," he said easily. "Having fun?"

As the two guys started chatting about some history final they'd taken the week before, Lisa sighed, almost wishing that Scott wasn't quite so friendly. *When Alex and I were together, he hardly took his attention off me long enough to notice anyone else,* she thought. *Scott doesn't exactly hide the fact that he likes me, but he's way too much of a social animal ever to be that totally focused on one person.*

Still, she couldn't help remembering the way Alex's devotion had sometimes gotten in the way. For instance, she doubted that someone like Scott would have had such a problem with her trip to California the previous summer. Alex's loneliness and jealousy had really been an issue between them for a long time. Thinking about that as she watched Scott turn to greet yet another friend, Lisa thought idly that it would be nice if there were a way to combine two people, taking the best qualities of each. Then she could have all the things she loved about Alex rolled together with the great qualities that intrigued her in Scott.

She almost giggled aloud at the thought. Obviously, she'd watched one too many late-night horror movies with Alex. It was ridiculous to try to imagine what some kind of mad-scientist version of the two guys would be like. Would she call him Scolex? Or maybe Alott? Either way, she was being a little unfair. Alex and Scott were both great guys, and she knew a lot of people would envy her, having to choose between them. Of course, that didn't mean it was going to be easy.

Not unless Mom makes the choice for me by making

me move to New Jersey, she thought, her stomach twisting into a knot as it always did when she thought about that particular topic. *Then I won't have either one of them—or any of my other friends, either.*

That thought was way too depressing for an otherwise beautiful Christmas Eve. Doing her best to squash it, she sipped her hot chocolate carefully and waited for Scott to finish his conversation.

Carole glanced over at Cam, who was riding beside her. Everyone was more subdued now that they were heading back to the stable, full of hot chocolate and holiday cheer. Carole and Cam were near the back of the group. The torchlight threw Cam's high cheekbones into sharp relief, making him look handsome and a little bit mysterious. Then he turned toward her. Catching her gaze, he smiled, and once again he was the old Cam, the Cam she was in love with.

"Having a good time?" he asked, reaching across the space between their horses to touch her leg.

She shivered slightly and returned his smile. "Uh-huh," she said. "Are you?"

"Definitely." Cam turned away for a moment as the horse he was riding, a sorrel gelding named Rusty, jigged slightly to the side.

Carole watched, admiring his riding skills. He

was a little out of practice, but she could tell that it was coming back to him with each ride they took together. Maybe someday soon he would decide he was ready for his own horse again. Maybe he would even board that horse at Pine Hollow so that he and Carole could ride together anytime they wanted. . . .

As she was imagining how wonderful that would be, Justine Harrington rode up beside her. "Hey, Carole," the younger girl said breathlessly. "What's the matter with Patch? He keeps trying to slow down when I make him trot."

Carole gave her a reassuring smile. "That's Patch for you," she said. "He knows he's been out for more than an hour, and he figures he's done his job, so he's being stubborn. Just keep giving your aids, and be as firm as you need to be about it." She pulled her riding crop out of her boot, knowing she wouldn't need it riding Calypso, who was always very forward on the trail. "Here, why don't you take this? You probably won't even need to use it. It'll be enough for him to know you have it. He should be fine once we get closer to the stable and he realizes he's headed back to his nice, cozy stall and a flake of hay."

As Justine thanked her and rode forward, looking relieved, Cam snorted. "These kids never run out of questions for you, do they? Any second now I'm expecting one of them to come over and ask which end of the horse goes forward."

"I don't mind." Carole smiled as she watched Justine lean forward to show the crop to her mount. "Even though I don't officially work at Pine Hollow right now, I guess the younger kids are used to coming to me with questions." She liked the feeling. It made her hopeful about the coming New Year, when she might be allowed to return to her job at the stable. She hadn't quite dared to bring it up with her father lately, but she could tell that he was pleased with her recent behavior and schoolwork.

Cam shrugged. "I know, I know. Still, I sort of wish we could sneak off and have our own private Starlight Ride without all the interruptions. So I could have you all to myself."

Carole smiled automatically, though she couldn't help thinking that Cam was sounding a little childish. What was the big deal? They were a couple—they could spend all the private time together they wanted. Tonight wasn't really about that. Yes, it was awfully romantic riding through the torchlit woods together. But part of what made it so magical was sharing it with all the other riders at Pine Hollow, even slightly bratty and impatient ones like Justine.

"Don't worry," she said lightly, not wanting Cam to guess what she was thinking. "We'll have plenty of time alone once you get back from your relatives' house next week."

Cam's face lit up. "Right," he agreed eagerly. "I

can't wait, especially for our gift exchange. Don't for-get—New Year's Eve afternoon, just you and me."

"I won't forget." Carole tried not to think about the fact that she still hadn't come up with any brilliant gift ideas. She was sure something would come to her soon.

Anyway, I probably shouldn't be getting so focused on the gift part of the exchange, she thought. *Because no matter what we get for each other, it's going to be really special just because we're together.*

She glanced over at Cam, realizing it was true. Cam probably wasn't going to get all hung up over a silly gift, and she shouldn't, either. That didn't mean she wasn't going to try to come up with something wonderful to show him how she felt. It just meant she realized it wasn't as important as feeling it.

How did I get so lucky, anyway? she wondered as he turned, caught her gaze again, and smiled at her. *Just when my whole life was on its way down the tubes, with the grounding and losing my job and the whole deal, Cam came along and made everything seem better. Just being with him like this, with all these other people around, makes me feel more alive.* She shuddered with happiness. *It makes me wish this wonderful, magical, special, romantic night would never end!*

FIFTEEN

Stevie peeked into the stall across from the wash stall at the end of the aisle. It was empty. "In here," she whispered, gesturing to Phil.

"Right behind you." Phil hoisted the large wrapped gift he was carrying onto one shoulder and followed her into the stall.

Moments later they were both seated on the clean-raked bare floor, knee to knee. Stevie glanced at the door, hoping they wouldn't be interrupted. She definitely didn't want anything to spoil their gift exchange. She wanted to savor how much Phil was going to love his gift. "Maybe we should try the loft instead," she said uncertainly.

"Forget it," Phil said with a laugh. "If we keep moving all over the stable this way, it'll be Ground-hog Day before we get around to exchanging gifts." He smiled and reached forward to brush a strand of hair off Stevie's forehead. "And I can't wait that long.

I'm dying to see how much you're going to love this." He patted the gift on his lap.

"Not as much as I'm dying to see how much you're going to love this," Stevie countered, holding up her own gift. She'd wrapped it carefully the night before in some pony-print wrapping paper she'd found at The Saddlery. It wasn't very Christmasy, but since Phil was half-Jewish anyway—not to mention more than half horse-crazy, just like her—Stevie figured it didn't matter that much.

"Okay, then, let's get started," Phil said. "First of all, merry Christmas." He leaned forward, grabbed her elbow, and pulled her toward him for a kiss.

Stevie kissed him back. "Merry Christmas and happy Hanukkah to you, too," she said. "Now go ahead and open it." She pushed the gift toward him.

"Okay. But you open yours first." Phil set his package in her lap.

"No, you first." Stevie hugged herself around the waist to stop herself from bouncing up and down with excitement.

Phil grinned. "How about if we both open them at the same time?"

"Well, okay." Stevie was tempted to insist once more that he go first, but she figured maybe that wasn't a good idea. Whatever he'd gotten her could only look pathetic after her amazing gift, and she didn't want to do that to him. Besides, she couldn't wait to see what was in the box he'd handed her. She loved presents. Ripping eagerly at the gold-and-white holiday paper, she soon recognized the red-and-white Saddlery box inside. She grinned. "Great minds think alike," she commented as Phil brushed away the pony paper and pulled out an almost identical box.

"I guess so." Phil winked. "What if we got each other the same thing?"

"I don't think that's going to happen," Stevie predicted confidently. She picked up her box and shook it. It was surprisingly heavy. "Anyway, this box is bigger than that one."

Phil started to lift the lid, then paused and glanced at her. "Count of three," he said.

Stevie nodded and got ready to lift her own lid. "One, two, three!"

She pulled up the lid and tossed it aside. Pushing past The Saddlery's logo-imprinted tissue paper, her hand brushed against soft but slightly rough-textured fabric. Puzzled, she peered at the mound of hunter-green wool nestled in the large box. Had Phil bought her a sweater, or perhaps a new hacking coat? He wasn't usually that interested in fashion, especially hers.

Meanwhile Phil was unfolding the chaps. He shook them out and stared at them. "Oh," he said.

"These are nice. Um, they look a little small, though."

"I know. But don't worry," Stevie put in eagerly. "The lady at the shop said you can exchange them with no problem. They're getting in a shipment next week, and they'll have all the sizes and colors then, so you can pick exactly which ones you want."

"Oh. That's great." Phil folded the chaps carefully and set them back in the box. Then he gestured to Stevie's box. "Aren't you going to unfold that and take a look?"

Stevie frowned slightly, puzzled by his lack of enthusiasm. "Don't you like the chaps?" she asked.

"Of course!" Phil reached over and squeezed her shoulder gently. "They're great. I just want to see what you think of your gift."

"Oh." Stevie realized she still wasn't sure what her gift was. Dumping the fabric out of the box onto her lap, she soon figured it out. "Oh, it's a turnout rug," she said blankly, wondering what on earth had possessed him to buy it for her. For one thing, it must have cost him a mint—she'd priced similar ones at The Saddlery in the past, and they cost even more than the chaps she'd bought him. Besides, her parents had bought her a nice fleece blanket for Belle just six months earlier on her birthday. "What a nice color," she added lamely, trying to muster some enthusiasm.

Phil peered at her quizzically. "What's wrong?" he asked. "Would you rather have a blue one? Because the sales guy said—"

"No, no, this is perfect," Stevie lied. She and Phil were usually honest with each other, but in this case she really didn't want to hurt his feelings, especially since he'd gone to so much expense. Besides, she supposed it wouldn't hurt Belle to have a spare rug. Maybe she could even sell the one her parents had bought. It hadn't cost as much as this one, but it might bring enough to make a down payment on a matching pair of those chaps for herself.

"Wait a minute," Phil said abruptly. "What's wrong with this picture?"

Stevie blinked, wondering if he'd read her thoughts. "What do you mean?" she asked cautiously.

Phil gestured to the horse blanket. "Okay, I'm no genius, but I can tell you're less than completely thrilled with your gift."

"No, really, I love it!" Stevie protested. "I—"

"Stow it," Phil interrupted bluntly, though he softened the comment with a smile. "I've known you a long time, Lake. And when you love something, you show it. And I don't mean by saying, 'Oh, what a lovely color.'" For the last sentence, he shifted into a falsetto.

Stevie rolled her eyes. "I didn't say it like that."

221

But this time her protest was halfhearted. She should have known better than to try to fool him. "But anyway, it's not like you're jumping up and down for joy about those chaps." She gestured at the pile of leather in his lap. "What's the matter? I was sure you'd love them."

"I do," Phil replied quickly. "Um, but why exactly did you think that?"

Stevie shrugged. "Because of what you said a while back when we were talking about Christmas," she said. "You were complaining about wearing holes in your jeans from riding so much. I thought it was, you know, a hint."

Phil glanced down at the chaps. "I said that?" He scratched his chin. "Oh. Well, I guess I wasn't really paying attention. Wasn't that the same day you kept mentioning how cold Belle was in her stall with winter coming on? Because that's what made me decide to get you the blanket."

Stevie tilted her head to one side, trying to remember herself saying that. A vague recollection of the conversation indicated that she might have said something to that effect. "I guess," she said slowly. "But I wasn't really thinking about Belle. I was thinking about how cold I'd been the last time I rode, even though I was wearing my warmest jeans and wool socks."

"Oh." Phil chewed his lower lip thoughtfully.

"Well, I guess I picked up on it because I'd just noticed Teddy shivering in his paddock the day before."

"Aha!" Stevie said, suddenly realizing what had happened. "So you bought *me* the gift that *you* were really hoping for."

"No, that's not it," Phil replied quickly. "I mean, maybe it's true that Teddy could use a warmer turnout rug. But I really thought you'd like it for Belle." He glanced down at the chaps he was still holding. "Besides, you did the same thing. You bought me the exact gift that you wanted."

"I think they're nice," Stevie protested. "But that doesn't mean I wanted them for myself."

Phil grinned and turned the label up to read it. "Oh, really?" he said. "Then why did you just happen to get them in *your* size?"

Stevie blushed, realizing it was true. "Oh, man," she said. "We're such losers! We both bought presents we wanted ourselves!"

They stared at each other for a second. Then, as if on cue, they burst into laughter.

"You're right," Phil gasped. "We *are* losers! But hey—at least now we can both have the gift we really wanted, right?"

Stevie nodded, still giggling. She piled the horse blanket back in its box and passed it to Phil. Phil passed her the box containing the leather chaps.

"Thanks," she said. "It's just what I always wanted."

"Me too." Phil grinned. "Thanks."

Stevie glanced at her watch and grimaced. "Oops, it's getting late," she said. "I want to find Carole and Lisa before they leave so I can give them their presents."

"Okay." Phil moved a little closer and leaned in to kiss her. "Just give me one last chance to say merry Christmas."

"Well," Lisa said, closing the stall door just in time to keep Eve from wandering out after her. Brushing off her hands, she turned to smile shyly at Scott. The evening seemed to be winding to a close, and she wasn't quite sure what came next. "This was fun."

"I had fun, too." Scott leaned one shoulder against the wall nearby, looking down at her steadily. "Thanks for agreeing to come with me."

"You're welcome. Thanks for asking."

Scott stood up straight and took a half step toward her, and Lisa braced herself for another mind-altering kiss. But instead, Scott just gazed at her seriously with his hands shoved in his pockets.

Finally he spoke. "I really like you, Lisa."

"I like you, too," Lisa began uncertainly. "Um, I just—"

But Scott cut her off with a raised hand. "Wait. There's more," he said soberly. "As I said, I really like you. But I know you still have feelings for Alex."

Lisa gulped. She wasn't sure what to say to that. "Well, we were together a long time," she murmured. "I guess, well, um . . ."

"I know." Scott smiled briefly. "Believe me, I understand. That's why I don't want to add to what you're going through right now by putting any pressure on you."

"What do you mean?" Lisa asked.

Scott took a deep breath. "I mean, I'm going to back off for a while," he said. "Give you some space to figure things out, decide who you really want to be with. You know where to find me if you want to, but I'm not going to be in your face anymore."

Lisa opened her mouth to respond, then closed it again. She wasn't sure whether she was more surprised, confused, or disappointed by what Scott was saying. *If he likes me as much as he claims, why would he do that?* she wondered. *I mean, Alex would never—*

She cut off the thought before she could finish it. Scott wasn't Alex, and Alex wasn't Scott. Wasn't that sort of the whole point?

"Okay," she told Scott softly. "Thanks for being so honest. I—I guess you're right. I'm not sure what I want to do right now."

Scott nodded. "Okay then," he said with another subdued smile. "Merry Christmas, Lisa."

"Merry Christmas," Lisa replied, feeling strangely unsettled as he turned and walked down the stable aisle without another word.

"Mmm," Cam murmured, burying his left hand in Carole's curly hair, which had come loose from its ponytail. "Now this is what I call a merry Christmas Eve." His right hand wrapped itself around her waist, then slid slightly lower as he pressed against her, pushing her against a soft pile of loose hay behind her.

Carole didn't answer. She was feeling too breathless. They had been making out since the moment they'd climbed into the hayloft for some privacy. It hadn't been long before things had gotten a little more intense than usual, though Carole wasn't quite sure how it had happened.

Still kissing him, she sat up a little straighter, dislodging Cam's wandering right hand in the process. Almost immediately, Cam rolled her over against another bale and slid his free hand under the hem of her sweater.

Carole froze. As Cam's hand continued to explore, she felt her heart starting to pound faster. Things were definitely starting to go further than usual. Gathering her wits, she shoved Cam away and sat up fast. "Stop," she blurted out.

"What's the matter?" Cam asked, sitting up and picking some hay out of his shirt collar. "Why did you stop? Is something wrong?"

Carole gasped for breath, trying to calm her racing heart. "It's—I just—we can't," she stammered. "I don't think we should, well . . ."

Cam blinked, looking confused. "I thought we were having a nice time," he said huskily, moving closer and taking her hand in his. "Weren't you having fun?"

"S-sure," Carole said uncertainly. "But things are moving, you know, kind of fast, and I'm not sure . . . Well, I'm not really sure I'm ready to, you know . . ."

"It's just that I'm going to miss you like crazy this next week, Carole." Cam's fingertip traced a pattern on her forearm, making her shiver. "I don't know if I can stand it."

"Oh." Carole gulped. "Uh, I'm going to miss you, too. I just . . ." Her voice trailed off as Cam bent over her, pressing his lips on hers once again.

"Carole! Yo, Hanson, where are you?" a voice called from somewhere below them.

Carole broke away, feeling strangely relieved. "Oops. That sounds like Stevie," she said, brushing

227

the hay off her clothes as she stood. "Um, I'd better go see what she wants."

Cam frowned. "Don't go," he said, standing and grabbing her around the waist. He buried his face in her neck, kissing her softly. "Please stay. Just for a little while longer."

"I can't." With a serious effort of will, Carole pushed him away again. "I'm sorry. I have to go. But we're still on for New Year's Eve, right?"

Cam sighed loudly, finally stepping back and shoving his hands in his pockets. "New Year's Eve," he said, his voice a bit sullen. "If I survive that long."

"Sorry." Carole stood on tiptoes and kissed him softly and quickly on the lips. "But I'll make it up to you then, I promise."

"Merry Christmas!" Stevie exclaimed breathlessly, peeking over the half door of Starlight's stall. "Sorry I'm late. I had to dig your gifts out of my cubby. They sort of fell down behind some other stuff."

"It's okay," Lisa said.

Carole smiled. "And a merry Christmas to you, too."

Stevie noticed that Lisa looked a little distracted, but she didn't comment on it. She had seen Scott leaving a couple of minutes earlier, and from the subdued expression on his face, she guessed that maybe the Starlight Ride hadn't been quite as romantic as he'd hoped. She couldn't help being relieved at that, though she felt a little guilty about it. Unlike Alex's new relationship—if one could call it that—with Nicole, it wasn't so easy to dismiss Scott's interest in Lisa. Stevie liked Scott, and she wanted him to be happy. But what if his happiness depended on taking Lisa away from Alex forever? What was she supposed to feel then?

Of course, it might not matter either way if Lisa's mother goes through with her crazy moving plan, she reminded herself with a flash of worry. *Let's just hope she gets over that whole thing soon, or Scott is going to be the least of our problems.*

She stepped aside as Carole and Lisa let themselves out of the stall, latching it behind them. The Starlight Ride had ended well over an hour before, and most of the other riders had already left to celebrate Christmas Eve with their families.

But the three friends had one more thing to do. "Ready to see your fabulous gifts?" Stevie asked them, thinking ruefully of her exchange with Phil. How had she let herself get so caught up in how great those chaps were that she'd totally missed the fact that Phil didn't really want them?

"Ready," Carole and Lisa said in unison.

Soon they were all seated cross-legged on the clean-swept floor of an empty stall. Each of them had brought gifts for the others. As they unwrapped the brightly wrapped packages and oohed and aahed over the contents—a sweatshirt for Carole from Lisa, a dressage video that Carole had chosen specially for Stevie, and more—Stevie thought once again of how silly she and Phil had felt after all their grand plans had turned out the way they had.

I guess I should have known better, she thought, holding out her arm so that Lisa could help fasten on the bracelet that was her gift. *The point isn't to spend a lot of effort picking out things. Things aren't really all that important. It's good friends that are the best gift of all, the one that keeps on giving.*

She smiled, wondering exactly when her own thoughts had started sounding like some kind of greeting card. But just because the sentiment was a little corny didn't mean it wasn't true. And Stevie was sure that, no matter what happened—with Scott and Alex, with Cam, with Lisa's mother's plans—that feeling would never go away. Not for the three of them.

"This is nice, isn't it?" she said suddenly, reaching out to envelop both of her friends in an impulsive hug. "Merry Christmas."

ABOUT THE AUTHOR

BONNIE BRYANT is the author of more than a hundred books about horses, including the Pine Hollow series, The Saddle Club series, The Saddle Club Super Editions, and the Pony Tails series. She has also written novels and movie novelizations under her married name, B. B. Hiller.

Ms. Bryant began writing The Saddle Club in 1986. Although she had done some riding before that, she intensified her studies then and found herself learning right along with her characters Stevie, Carole, and Lisa. She claims that they are all much better riders than she is.

Ms. Bryant was born and raised in New York City. She still lives there, in Greenwich Village, with her two sons.